Brand New Music

By Kyle Draper

"Surely, whoever speaks to me in the right voice, him or her I shall follow"

-Walt Whitman

Part One

Sean

Fall had arrived in Burnsville. This was about the time when the leaves on the trees began to change color and the weather became bearable. After an unusually grueling hot summer where temperatures reached over ninety degrees, it's nice to walk outside the door and not have sweat at once running down your arms and legs. With fall comes the rain. When the streetlights reflect off the leaves gently kissed with the moisture of a late evening shower. You could go to bed staring at a lush reddish-orange maple, then wake up the next morning to see that same tree bare. Just walking down, the street, and hearing the crunching of the leaves under your feet awakens something inside of you. It would seem as though the arrival of fall was a treat for everyone. Summer days, summer nights were in the past. This was a welcoming departure.

Burnsville was a very liberal, progressive town that has grown from creativity and free-thinking. It's common to go to downtown Burnsville and feel as if you were in a smaller version of New York, Boston, or even Chicago. Downtown thrives with fresh faces, young and old, who want to experience what the town has to offer. The streets were filled with bars, coffee shops, furniture studios, restaurants, art studios, galleries, and bakeries. She puts you under her spell and has you coming back for more. Tourists have made Burnsville a permanent residence. Those who were just passing through town to get to the next big city never make it. The possibilities here are endless. Musicians, painters, and writers have found refugees here. You can see their work on display throughout the town, on the side of buildings, sidewalks, and even in local shop windows. There's nothing better than window shopping with a little culture. Downtown and on the west side is where you could experience this artistic flare the most.

Sean Donovan lived right in the heart of downtown in an old apartment building that was built in the 1940s. As he walked home from work during nature's metamorphosis, he pulled up the collar on his wool coat protecting his neck and walked briskly to the steps of his apartment building. After kicking some leaves from the foot of the door, he opened the door and entered the building. His apartment was on the fourth floor. He didn't take the elevator this time. He decided to take the stairs instead. As he walked down the hallway, he shivered from the chill of the night air and put his key into apartment 4G.

Sean was lucky to find this apartment. It was a two-bedroom one-bath with hardwood floors and a huge kitchen. It had great views of the downtown skyline from the living room and dining room, the mountains from the bedroom and it was rent-controlled. As he stood in the atrium, he noticed the blinds on the living room and dining room windows were slightly open so that the moonlight could sneak in and outline everything from the furniture to the appliances. The light to accent the art pieces on the walls. Some of the pieces were from world-famous artists while others were by local artists. The pieces by local artists were Sean's favorite. Most of them were a gift from his friend, Michelle Rockwell, who worked at an art gallery on the west side of town. He dropped his keys on the dark wood end table, walked into the living room taking off his coat, and threw it across the recliner on his way to the kitchen.

Sean was in his early twenties, six feet two inches tall with very handsome dark features and light grey eyes. His father, who left him and his mother when he was five, was of French-Canadian descent. His grandparents were from Montreal and still live there. His father went to college in Colorado where he met Sean's Irish-German mother. She was a theater major and he was an economics major. Two years after they met, they were married and moved to Burnsville a year later. Sean's mother worked in the local theater house downtown, acting, and doing some production work where his father had a very difficult time finding work. After Sean was born, his father found it more difficult to support his family and be there as a loving, supporting father and husband. After many tumultuous fights, he left, leaving a young actress to raise a son on her own. Sean would not hear from his father again until his high school graduation and even then, Sean never forgave the man that left his mother crying in her pillow night after night.

Sean attended The University of Burnsville as a sophomore. He wasn't sure what he wants to study but had been taking a lot of writing courses. He worked at the local newspaper nights during the week and on the weekends. An avid reader, he had two bookshelves full of books he has read from when he was in middle school to present. His mother hoped he would be interested in becoming an actor and studying theater. Sean's early years were very theatrical being exposed to the arts at a very early age. His creative side did come out in high school, but not towards the theater. Writing was his passion. His mother kept the countless short stories and poems he had written over the years. She would find him in his room reading book after book while other teenagers his age were outside climbing trees, riding their bikes all over town, or playing basketball. The bookshelves take up most of the living room from floor to ceiling. His friends would tease him about opening a bookstore in his apartment for extra income.

Before he got to the kitchen, Sean noticed the blinking light from his answering machine. As he stood there for a moment, his eyes did a quick scan of the apartment. He then hit the play button on the machine. Sean never made it to the kitchen. As the message played, he turned and stumbled down the hallway to the bedroom. The second bedroom across the hall he used as an office. As he went into the bedroom, he turned on the light and noticed the closet door open, several dresser drawers' open, and missing items from on top of the entertainment center. He continued to stumble towards the bed and fell back upon it. He stared blankly into the ceiling fan rotating above him. He remained perfectly still just staring at the fan while his light grey eyes became heavy with tears falling down the sides of his face.

Hours had passed, and Sean was no longer lying on the bed. In the background, you could hear the message repeating on the machine. He was in his underwear standing in front of the mirror in the bathroom. With both hands on the sink, he leaned in closer examining his red, flushed face. He took a serious look at every feature and every mark. He made different facial expressions, even an angry one that is photographed in his mind. He then really looked into his reddish-grey eyes that still had tears masking them. His anger had turned into sadness. He stepped back and extended his left arm, picked up the knife he laid on the sink, and put it to his wrist. He looked into the mirror again and noticed his eyes and face became unrecognizable. With tears still running down his face, he held the knife unsteadily on his wrist. The howling wind outside seems to be in harmony with the message on the machine consuming the apartment and Sean's mind. On the shelf above the toilet, the cordless phone rang quietly.

As the ringing continued, they grew louder. Sean snapped out of his trance and dropped the knife in the sink after nicking his wrist. A droplet of blood ran down his wrist, found its path down the lines of his hand, and fell into the sink next to the knife. Without taking his eyes from himself in the mirror, he reached for the phone knocking over a few items that fell on the toilet seat lid before hitting the floor. Finally getting a grasp on the phone after ringing continuously, he answered. The voice on the other end called out without a response from Sean. Only after a few minutes did he finally speak to the person on the other end of the phone. "It's over…"

Several hours later, Sean reluctantly got dressed and met his friend, Lauren, at the downtown bar, Midnights. Midnights was a local bar where a lot of college students, teacher's assistants, and professors frequent for some drink specials and decent food. It was typical to see graduate students and professors sharing ideas and knowledge over several pitchers of beer and nachos. Midnights weren't known for the cuisine, but the happy hour specials. Midnights was more of a lounge than your typical bar or nightclub. They had a lounge area with a main bar and tables for those who want to enjoy a nice lunch or dinner. Attached by a hallway, several restrooms, and storage rooms, the other side of Midnights had bar tables, a smaller bar, and a stage with a medium-size dance floor. Local bands and jazz musicians usually tried to find some following there and were usually successful, depending on how many times a week they would perform there.

Sean and Lauren sat in one of the booths in the main room. All the booths opposite the bar were dim-lit. The seats and table are a very dark, thick wood texture. Lauren and Sean met at the university. They had one independent study course together. Lauren was a senior when Sean was a first-year student.

Lauren Capshaw was a fashion editor for the local newspaper that Sean worked for. Her position at the paper explained her very stylish, confident attitude. She was short, about five feet three inches tall, tan complexion, mostly from hours of sunbathing, but also because she was Italian. She had blonde straight hair that came down to her surgically altered breasts. She can be cold at times to those she doesn't know but can also be a cold-hearted bitch to those she knew all too well. She noticed Sean staring out the window barely talking or looking at her. Lauren, wearing a short purple cocktail dress with gold high heels, reached in her purse to get her Camel Lights. Lauren can't seem to have one drink without having ten cigarettes. She lit a cigarette and blew the smoke at Sean to get his attention. "What do you mean 'it's over'"? Lauren said.

"Jaime dumped me." Sean turned to Lauren as he finished his beer.

"You're kidding me?"

"Nope. He dumped me tonight." Sean stared into his empty glass as he traced his finger around the rim.

"Let me take care of that for you." Lauren got the attention of the server. The server came over to the table and she ordered another round of drinks. Sean chuckled and gave the server the empty glass. "I don't need any more to drink."

"It's exactly what you need right now."

After a few moments, the server returned to the table with another round of drinks. Lauren was drinking a vodka martini with three olives and Sean was drinking draft beer. Lauren put out her cigarette and immediately lit another one before her drink hit the table.

"What I need is to know is what the hell happened? Suddenly, the love I thought I had is gone just like that." Sean told Lauren.

"What is the big deal?! It was your first relationship! First relationships don't last forever. Just think of this as a learning experience. I may not be an expert on relationships, but I do know when they are over, they are just that…. over! You will meet someone else, someone new."

"Oh please! You date men, get what you want, and then leave them with a wet-nap and pop tart while showing them the door! Plus, this is not about the relationship! I'm referring to the love we shared for one another. That was something special to me; at least I thought it was something special to him too."

Lauren took a big gulp of her martini and ate the olives, "Love sucks, baby, and the sooner you realize that, the better!"

"That's nice, thanks a lot," Sean remarked sarcastically. Sean rested his chin in his hands and sighed. He barely drank his beer but continued to play with the rim of the glass with his finger.

"Give it time. This too shall pass," Lauren quipped.

"What am I going to do while I'm just giving it time?"

"Well first, you're going to have to find a place to live because you can't live there with Jaime anymore. We'll go get your stuff. You can stay with me for as long as you want."

"Not necessary," he sighed.

"Why?"

Sean took several gulps from his beer and exhaled, "Because when I got home from work, the drawers were empty. His clothes and shoes were gone from the closet and the video game console was gone. He left, and I have no idea where he went."

Lauren seemed to muster up some resemblance of shock, "What?!"

Sean began to stare off as his eyes became watery and full of tears, "He left me a message on the answering machine telling me that our relationship was over."

Lauren finished her drink and signaled to the server for another round.

"He was so cold," he continued with a tremor in his voice, "There was no feeling. No apologetic tone. There was nothing. I played the message over and over. Do you remember that recliner we bought at the flea market?"

She shook her head in acknowledgment. The server brought over another fresh round of drinks.

"I sat in it and kept listening to that message," he said.

Lauren took a sip of her drink and started to giggle, "You're starting to sound like a soap opera." She began to laugh as Sean looked at her stone-faced.

"I almost did it, you know. I went into the bathroom and almost did it. I seriously thought about it. I stood there staring at myself in the mirror. How pathetic, right? I got a knife from the kitchen and put…."

Lauren continued to laugh at Sean, "Ok, now I know this is a soap opera!"

Sean became very defensive. "I'm glad you find my pain so fucking amusing! I'm sitting here telling you that I thought about killing myself and you're cracking jokes?! This break up had me contemplating taking my own life! Still, think it's funny?! Still want to crack jokes?!"

Lauren pulled out another cigarette from the pack. "Yes, I do because it's stupid! He's not worth killing yourself over!"

"Well, I didn't do it, did I?!"

They sat there for a moment in uncomfortable silence. Sean looked out the window again as people passed by. He noticed a couple sitting on the bench across the street kissing. They looked so happy and in love with one another. He sighed deeply and turned away from the window. Lauren took a drag of her cigarette and sipped of her drink. Sean finished off his beer and took a sip of the fresh one in front of him. Lauren exhaled her cigarette but this time away from Sean.

"Look, I'm sorry. I didn't mean to take your situation lightly. I just know you to be smarter than that and I know you realize that this is something not to hurt yourself over!"

"It's alright," he sighed. "Thanks for being here to listen. I'm glad you called because I don't know what I would have done if that ringing didn't snap me out of doing something really stupid."

They both smiled and raise their glasses to toast. They cheered, and both drank. Lauren finished her drink in a matter of moments while Sean took his time but didn't finish his beer. Lauren took a drag from her cigarette and flicked the ashes in the ashtray.

"Find a roommate!" exhaled Lauren.

"I don't think I could handle someone else in that space with me."

"Can you afford the apartment's rent and utilities by yourself?"

"No…"

"Then it looks like you're finding yourself a roommate!"

Sean picked up the menu on the table and began to flip through it. Not sure if he was hungry or trying to avoid this conversation, but it didn't seem to work since the conversation continued with or without him. "Who would I get to move in with me? Everyone I know either has their place or already has roommates."

Lauren grabbed the menu from Sean and put it down on the table. "What about Dave? You told me that he was looking for a new place. I think he would enjoy living downtown."

"Dave already lives downtown---with Mark!"

Lauren put out her cigarette. Seeming a little uncomfortable, she tried to compose herself quickly. "Ahem. Dave is still seeing Mark?"

"Well, yes, I figured you would know that since Mark *is* your brother!"

Sean finished his beer and took the menu again to look at. "They've been together for a couple of years now."

Lauren snatched the menu from Sean and looked at it. The server came back over to her, "Did you want to order something?"

"Sweetie, I will not be eating anything but the olives in my martini in which I'm fresh out. Now, how can we, meaning you, fix this for me?" she asked holding the empty martini glass up to the server.

"Um, actually, I would like to order a house salad with bleu cheese dressing and an order of wings...medium, please." Sean interrupted.

The server smiled in acknowledgment of Sean and took the menu away from Lauren. "I was certain that Dave would have dumped his ass by now. I mean, he's a doctor and my brother is just a writer."

"He's not just a writer. He's a *very* successful writer. Two books on the New York Times bestseller list is important. What is it you have against your brother?"

The server returned to the table with another round of drinks and Sean's salad.

"Whatever." she sighed.

"Okay, so you had a little bit of a crush on Dave and it didn't work out."

"Of course, it didn't work out because the man is GAY!"

"Don't forget in love with your brother!" Sean laughed.

Lauren rolled her eyes and drank her embarrassment away. The details of how Sean and Lauren "officially" met might be a little fuzzy in her mind, but it might have something to do with her crush on Sean's older cousin, David. Sean used to party with David when he was in high school. He felt important and popular because he was going to college parties when he was only a first-year student. Sean met Lauren at one of these parties and remembered how Lauren would make eyes at his cousin and flirt with him. David never seemed interested which made her want him more. Nothing ever came of it. Sean didn't see or hear from Lauren again until college.

"It won't last," Lauren sulked.

"They've been together for two years now! Accept it!"

"Whatever! Just put the damn ad in the newspaper and find a roommate!"

Sean giggled and started to eat his salad. Before he ate it, he picked out the croutons and put them on a napkin. He meant to tell the server that he didn't want croutons in his salad but was distracted by Lauren's rant to get a new drink. He just wanted to get his order in before she began to piss off their server. Sean was only able to take a few bites of his salad before his wings arrived. "I'll do it tomorrow."

"There you go. So, have you told Dave about the breakup?"

"No. He'd probably be thrilled."

"Why would he be happy about that?" she asked slightly confused.

"Dave never liked Jaime. He felt I could do better."

"True," said under her breath.

"I heard that!"

Sean finished his salad and began eating his wings when Lauren lit up another cigarette. "I meant you to!" Lauren ate the olives in her empty glass. She looked at her watch and realized what time it was. With that expression after looking at her watch, you would think she had a hot date or one-night stand with a vodka or Camel lights sales representative.

"Oh shit. I got to get going!

She got the attention of the server and signaled for the check. With a little bit of attitude towards her, she brought over the check. Sean looked at her with a mouth full of wings and wing sauce all over his fingers. "What? I'm not even done eating here."

"I'm sorry but I have to run! I'll pay for the drinks…and your food." Lauren dropped her credit card on top of the check and motioned for the server to take it away. The server snatched both and snarled at Lauren. She looked over to Sean, "Is there anything else you need, sweetie?"

"No thank you."

The server left and didn't even acknowledge Lauren.

"I hope that bitch doesn't think she's getting a tip."

"Stop it. I'll leave the tip."

The server returned with credit card slips and a pen. She gave Lauren a fake smile and wished Sean a good night. Lauren signed the slips, leaving no tip and got her coat and purse.

"Listen, don't forget to put that ad in the paper. Hey, I'm very sorry about what Jaime did to you, but believe me, you will get through this. Things will get better and you will find someone again. I promise."

"Thanks, but what if I still want the old someone back, Lauren?"

Lauren got up from the booth and walked over to Sean's side, leaned over and kissed him on the head. "Um, no. Time to move on, baby!"

"Bye," Sean sighed.

Lauren walked out of the bar as if she was walking down the catwalk. Sean finished his wings and beer. He sat there for a moment and realized that he was alone again. After a year of being somebody's somebody, he was suddenly nobody's somebody. He was consumed by his thoughts once more. His smile was gone. He began to slowly turn back to face the window with caution. He wouldn't be able to take another romantic scene to this emotional drama that had closed in his heart. As he stared out the window, he saw his present. It had fallen from the branches and to the ground just like the leaves; blown away by the wind or simply stepped on. The fall was here.

Johnny

Like other musicians, Johnny and Seth felt right at home in Burnsville. They put a band together, found gigs, a local following, friends and even girlfriends. They were at the top and not taking anything for granted. They skated around downtown, really got into buying vintage art, and updated their sleeves with new and exciting designs.

They were downtown coming from the tattoo shop. Johnny wore a blue jean jacket with a logo tee underneath and cargo shorts with Chuck Taylors while Seth sported a vintage tee with a light multi-colored scarf, jeans, and boots. They had tattoos all over their legs and arms. Johnny had a few on his chest and Seth had two on his back. Most of the tattoos have to do with their love of music, the ocean, and graffiti art. After walking for some time, they found a bench next to the park to relax. Johnny handed Seth the college newspaper from his backpack with an ad circled.

"You found a place! That's great, man! Where is it?".

"Those apartments down off Jefferson and Belvedere."

"Wait, the apartments with the lion statues at the entrance of the building?"

"Yeah."

Seth whistled, "Those are some nice apartments…and you found it in the college paper?"

"Yeah. I was looking for longboard and saw the ad."

"One bedroom or two?"

"Two bedrooms. The ad said looking for a roommate, so I called. The guy's name is Sean. His last roommate moved out suddenly about a month ago."

"Suddenly? What's that all about?" Seth inquired.

"I don't know. It's none of my business and I wasn't about to ask." He said.

"Sounds suspicious to me. Some investigating might be needed."

Johnny laughed, "You're always suspicious of everyone and everything."

"I can't help it. I'm a cautious person. I just don't want to wake up one morning, read the paper to find that you were discovered chopped up in this man's freezer!"

"Neurotic is more like it."

"Whatever you want to call it, I'm just concerned about you."

"I appreciate that. That's why you're my best friend."

"And as your best friend, it's my job to worry and be concerned."

Johnny and Seth met six years ago at a battle of the bands in New York. Seth played guitar for one of the bands battling. They both got to talking and Seth learned that Johnny was also a musician. If you were to ask him, he would tell you he was more of a singer and songwriter. He did play guitar but enjoyed singing and writing more. Johnny was really into music and art. He was not only an excellent musician but a very promising graffiti artist. Originally from California, Seth Rosen used to surf and was a professional skater when a knee injury ended his career years prior. He moved out to New York and started playing guitar in a band shortly after.

Johnny Forman was born and raised in Yonkers, New York. He had short hair, six feet tall, dark in complexion, and wore Buddy Holly type glasses. To look at him, you would automatically think he was Caucasian with a damn good tan, but ethically, Johnny was Italian and Portuguese; which gave him a very sexy and exotic look. He refused to wear contacts, but his glasses didn't take away from his very rugged good looks; not to mention his very deep, vibrant brownish-green eyes. Seth had shaggy, curly hair, six feet three inches tall, light tan complexion, and had a beard. Johnny was in his mid-twenties and Seth was a few years older. Seth was slender and athletic as Johnny was average in build yet possessed a toned muscular physique. This came from years of running around the streets of New York and playing basketball in the neighborhood. Girls and some guys alike found Johnny completely adorable. His cuteness would usually come with a bit of shyness, but Seth was nowhere close to being shy. Very outspoken and willing to tell you how he felt and what was on his mind. Women wanted to cuddle and take care of Seth. With Johnny, it was purely sexual.

Johnny took the paper away from Seth and flipped through it. Seth looked at Johnny as if he had something to say but was afraid to say it. He looked up at the sky, and then closed his eyes with a few deep breaths and decided to say something, "Hey, I need to tell you something."

Johnny continued to flip through the paper, "What's up?"

Seth took another deep breath before saying anything, "Natalie called me last night."

Johnny closed the paper with his eyes completely fixated at the ground. Natalie was Johnny's girlfriend until a month ago. They had a happy and loving relationship for three years. They met at one of their shows. After their set, Johnny and Natalie sat at the bar for hours just talking, laughing, and even crying about things they had been through in their lives. After that night, they were inseparable. They went out to romantic dinners, took long walks downtown, and had amazing sex morning, noon, and night. Johnny's music had a different sound to it ever since they started dating. It was still good as before but there is something different, something new and exciting. Whatever is it, the band and their fans loved it. A month ago, it all ended. Johnny had been living on Seth's couch ever since the breakup. Seth was not thrilled with Johnny's possessions collecting in his living room turning *his* place into *their* place but realized this was a tough time for him and what was important now was being there for him. Johnny stood up and started to walk away.

Seth got up and grabbed Johnny by the arm and tried to stop him, "Did you hear what I said?"

Johnny snatched his arm away from Seth, "I heard you," Johnny upset, "What the hell did she want? Better yet, why's she calling you?"

Johnny and Seth walked up to another bench in the park next to a fountain and sat down. Seth took his guitar from his back and played a few chords. Johnny looked at Seth as he waited for him to answer his question, "Hello? Why's she calling you?"

Seth stopped playing chords, "She called me because she's worried about you. She misses you. She wants to talk to you to tell you how sorry…."

"Hey, she fucked up! Her apologies don't mean shit!"

Seth sat his guitar down. He put his hand on Johnny's shoulder and tried to show a little support. "Man, we all make mistakes. She seems sincere in wanting to make things better and work it out. I think you should…."

Johnny got defensive and stood up, "Seth! When you catch your girlfriend in the arms of another man, come and talk to me. Until then, I wish you would stay the fuck out of it!"

Johnny started to leave again. Seth grabbed his guitar and tried to stop him, but this time he got a little physical with Seth and pushed him, "Johnny! Stop! Look at yourself! You're drinking all the time! No one sees you anymore! You were just about to kick my ass for no reason! What's going on with you? What's happening? Where's your music?"

Johnny stepped back and pointed at Seth, "Don't you fucking start with me about that music shit! When I'm ready to play music, *my* music, then I'll play *my* music… so just back off!" Johnny took a deep breath and sat back down, this time on the steps of the fountain. "I'm just not inspired, alright?!"

Seth sat down next to Johnny and exhaled, "It's okay, Johnny…I get it, but you are in the shits right now. You're pissed off at the world. Johnny, this puts you at your creative peak, man."

Johnny, still upset, looked at Seth with a straight face. Seth made a silly facial expression that made him laugh changing the entire mood of the conversation.

"So, do you want to check out my new place? I can move in next week once I pay the deposit." Johnny said.

"When?"

"How about now? We can go and check it out. I can text Sean to see if he's home."

"I can't. Kelly and I are having dinner with some friends, but I will be more than happy to help you get moved in."

"Damn, really want to get rid of me that bad, huh?"

"I want my couch back! It's starting to smell too much like you."

Johnny punched Seth in the arm, and he pushed Johnny back. They laughed, and both got up from the steps to walk back towards downtown. Seth grabbed his guitar and started to play more chords, humming a little song. Johnny silently walked next to him.

The next day, Lauren was sitting on her bed wearing a white robe drinking a glass of wine. She had the bottle sitting on the floor next to her nightstand. She reached over to her nightstand, where an erotic picture of her lying across a bed of satin seductively wearing only black lacey underwear, sat in an ivory frame, picked up her cordless phone and called Sean. She admired her fingernails as she waited for Sean to answer.

Sean was in the kitchen washing dishes in the tank top and sweatpants when the phone rang. He turned off the water, dried his hands, and ran to catch the phone before the answering machine picked up.

"Hello?" Sean answered.

"So, has he moved in yet?"

"Next week."

"Are you excited?"

"About?"

"Getting a roommate!"

Sean sighed, "I still think it's too soon, but I can't afford the rent and utilities alone. I guess I'm going have to get ready and excited." Sean walked around the living room until his attention was drawn to the recliner that remained the only symbol of a failed relationship in the apartment. Sean walked over to the chair cautiously and sat in it and exhaled. Lauren continued talking on the other end, but he didn't appear to hear a single word.

To look at her apartment, you would think it was decorated by Pier One Imports. Everything in her apartment, from the dishes to the rugs, was white; eggshell white. She had huge portraits of herself in every room except for the bathroom. Above her tub was a portrait of her and four male A&F models, all wearing nothing but khaki shorts, violating Lauren wearing very short, cut-off shorts with a strappy mid-drift gray shirt. One of the models was cupping her breast, while the other had his hand in her crotch. One model was pulling back her hair and licking her face and the last model had his mouth on the back of that model's neck with his arm across his chest.

Sean rubbed the arms of the chair, leaned back, and began to sob quietly. Lauren called out several times to Sean. "Hello? Sean?"

"Ahem. Yes. I'm here. Sorry. Everything's going to be fine."

"What's wrong with you? You sound funny."

Sean curled up in the chair and sobbed even harder. "I miss him, Lauren. I miss…."

"Sean!" Lauren yelled.

Sean sobbed, "I know, I know. It's over. I need to get over it, but I can't help it."

"I know it's hard. It's only been a month and moving in together must be…"

Lauren paused and realized she might have said something that she shouldn't. Sean stopped crying long enough to catch a little of what she said and was curious to know what she meant. "What? What moving in? Who's moving where?"

"Oh shit…"

"Lauren…what moving in?"

Lauren sat up on the bed and grabbed her glass of wine from the nightstand. "Listen, don't get mad, but after the breakup, Jaime…. They had been seeing one another for months now. I'm sorry."

"Wait! How do you know all this?!" Sean shouted.

"Jaime told me…"

Furious, Sean stood up from the recliner, walked over to the window, and wiped his face with his hand. "Wait a second…are you telling me that you knew this entire time that Jaime was cheating on me…for months?!"

"Well…"

Sean pissed, "Well, what?! You knew this entire time and didn't say shit to me?! I thought we were friends?!"

"I know it's hard when you realize you've been cheated on…."

"No! I'm not referring to that! I'm referring to the fact that you sat there, listened to my sob story knowing Jaime had cheated on me! Come to think of it, you knew that he moved out with this guy! So, who is he? You know what doesn't matter…. How could you do this to me?!" Sean yelled.

"Sean, I'm sorry. I am, but it's hard being friends with both of you."

"Well, that's a relief. At least I know where your loyalty lies."

Lauren finished her glass of wine, reached down to the floor, and picked up the bottle to refill her glass. She lit one of her cigarettes and set it in the ashtray on the table. "Look, I was trying to be there for you." She remarked coldly.

"I'm so stupid."

"Sean."

"Fuck you, Lauren! And fuck our friendship!"

Lauren spits out her wine on her new very white rug.

"What?!"

"I said, fuck you and don't ever call or speak to me again!" Sean hung up the phone.

Lauren dropped the phone on her lap and sat there. She then dialed a number and waited for an answer. Her voice was shaken and low.

"Ahem. We need to talk…he knows."

Sean turned from the window and threw the phone on the recliner. He walked through the living room swearing and swinging in the air. He then stopped and went into the kitchen. He came back to the living room holding a knife, the same one he was holding a month ago, and violently stabbed the recliner repeatedly. Jab after jab, he plunged the knife deeper and deeper into the recliner, crying and cursing with every strike. He dropped to his knees to the floor as the knife fell out of his hand sliding across the hardwood floor under the dining room table. Sean sat there covered in the guts of the recliner sobbing. The recliner resembled not only a failed relationship but Sean's heart.

Coffee Talk

The next day, Sean met his cousin, David, for coffee at Writer's Wall, a café in West Burnsville. West Burnsville is better known as the art district. A lot of artists that live in the area have their art studios lining the streets along with many cafés with good coffee and great food. Most of these cafes have the artwork of local artists hanging on their walls. Most of them are for sale and most of them belong to the artists who either own the café or work there. Along with the cafes and studios, there were also plenty of shops, owed by the artist selling their stuff to those visiting the area that would like to take a souvenir home to the big city. When you walk into these shops, you can't help but smell Nag Champa with a slight hint of patchouli in the air. It is very intoxicating.

Sean sometimes wished he lived in West Burnsville and hoped to move there one day. There is a rift with young professionals and college students who can't decide on whether to live in the happening day and nightlife of downtown Burnsville or the much laid back and artsy West Burnsville. Either way, both are great places to live and can be pricey; especially if you plan to live there alone.

David was a pediatrician at the local hospital. David and Sean have always been close even though David was older. Sean always saw David as a big brother rather than a cousin. David used to protect Sean when he started high school since he was a senior, so Sean wasn't bullied by the upper-class students because they knew he was David's cousin.

A year later, David was off to college, and Sean had proven himself enough in school that most of his friends were now juniors and seniors. David would take Sean to college parties on the weekends and spent most of his free time with him; bowling, playing pool, going to movies, and hanging out at bookstores. Sean didn't even feel uncomfortable or weird when David came out of the closet in his second year of med school. David's parents took it hard at first, but soon got passed it and supported him.

David's aunt, Sean's mother, was always there for him. She was like a second mom to him. He came out to her one night when he was struggling with who he was. Being in the theater all her life, she was very open-minded and had plenty of good friends who are gay. Her best friend is a lesbian and was more than happy to be the maid of honor at her wedding to her partner of twenty-three years. By the time David announced he was gay, Sean had graduated from high school and it didn't matter to him. To him, David meant everything.

"Can you believe her?" Sean asked.

David handed him his coffee and sat down. "I can't believe either one of them."

"What a bitch!" Sean took a sip of his coffee.

"Ha, which one?"

"Err, I'm just so angry!"

David sipped his coffee, "What did you expect? Lauren just happens to be friends with both of you. It was only a matter of time before someone would get screwed in all of the this....no pun intended."

"If everything was so good between us or at least I thought, why cheat? I never realized or even imagined this would happen."

David crossed his arms and leaned back in his chair. "Who does?! Maybe he wasn't satisfied with being with just one person."

"Okay, let's just say that's the case, why not work it out? Why not come up with a solution? Why make cheating the only option?"

"That might not have been your first choice, but it was his. Then again, you're not Jaime. And let me just say, we're all thankful for that!"

"Okay, could you at least pretend to be concerned with the fact that I'm hurting here? I'm still in love with him."

David sighed, "Alright, but that the ship has sailed and will not be returning to dock."

They took a moment to sit back and enjoy their coffee. Sean wondered for a moment.

"Ahem...Dave, do you think I should...."

"No!" David said sharply.

"You don't even know what I was going to say?!"

"Go ahead. Say what you were going to say."

"Well, do you think I should try to...."

"No!" David repeated.

"What?"

"Look, I'm just going to say this once. There's nothing to work out or try to fix here! It's done! Over! Finished!

"I get it, but we all make mistakes. We give second chances just as long as those mistakes aren't repeated, right?"

"Normally I would agree with you, but this is one mistake that can't be fixed because I'm telling you it will be repeated."

"What makes you an expert?" Sean said defensively.

"Please don't let me state the obvious," David scoffed. "I'm older and have been through a lot more heartache than you, my friend."

"I know, but Jaime was all I knew."

"So, get to know someone else!"

"That's helpful, thanks." Sean sighed.

"Always here to help," David laughed. "I'm sorry, but sometimes the truth hurts."

"You know what else hurts, not having the support and understanding of your friends and family!"

David sipped his coffee but then slammed down his cup. "Don't give me that shit! I've always been there for you and supported you no matter what you did or who you dated, but I'll be damned if I'm going to sit here and insist that you work things out, so you can get hurt and played again! Doing so would show you that I don't give a shit! I give a shit! You got me?!" David calmed down and reached for Sean's hand. Sean smiled with a sense of reassurance from the man that has always been there and protected him from harm. David let go of Sean's hand and noticed the entertainment magazine on the table. This gave him an idea that could be useful to Sean. "Have you thought about placing a personal ad, Sean?"

"Umm, I'm not ready for that."

"It could be good for you...allowing you to get to know someone new. Move on and move forward. Get past all this shit and stop obsessing about Jaime."

"I'm not obsessing. It's only been a month for crying out loud."

"Well, that's long enough if you ask me."

Mark arrived looking very GQ wearing a black V-neck t-shirt with a sports jacket, jeans, and Kenneth Cole loafers. David stood up to greet him with a hug and kiss. Mark took off his sunglasses and sat next to David.

David met Mark at this very café. Mark moved to the United States from England three years ago, just around the time they met. Mark is Lauren's brother but grew up in England with their father when their parents divorced when Mark was eight and Lauren was six. Their meeting was something that could have been written by Mark himself. Mark had ordered a coffee-to-go while David was coming in to do the same thing before his shift started. They were waiting for their coffees when they both reached for the same cup. When their eyes met, it was love at first sight. Mark not only had smoldering good looks and intellect but a killer British accent underneath his soft-spoken demeanor.

"Sorry I'm late...lunch ran long with my parents." Mark said.

"It's okay, baby. We were just sitting here talking about life and love."

"Hmm...sounds interesting."

"Believe me, it's not," Sean said drinking the rest of his coffee.

David tried changing the subject by addressing Mark.

"So how long is your father in town?"

"He leaves tomorrow night. He's going to France before heading back to England. You know, I do miss it there, but wouldn't trade my life here for anything."

"Looks like you're stuck in the States with me."

"I wouldn't have it any other way, baby."

David and Mark kissed. Sean looked at them disgusted and crossed his arms. "Ugh. Do you mind?"

David turned from kissing Mark addressing Sean. "Oh, don't hate!"

Mark reached out to Sean across the table. "Are you sure you're okay?"

"We've been talking about Jaime," David said.

"What the bloody hell for?" Mark said disgustedly.

"What...." Sean shocked.

"I'm sorry, mate, but Jaime is a complete arsehole!"

"We already covered that too," David remarked.

"You know, it's funny how all this is coming out now. Where were you guys when we were together?"

"Oh, we couldn't tell you then. You were so happy and so in love," David mentioned.

"And now?"

"Well, you're not so happy..."

"...And not so much in love," Mark added.

Sean exhaled and scratched his head, "I don't believe this."

Mark suddenly got an idea. "You know, it wouldn't kill you to put a personal...."

"No!" Sean bellowed.

"What?"

"We covered that too," David said. "Listen, you need to stop letting this consume you. You are having someone move in with you next week, Johnny, right? Concentrate on that. Don't worry about Jaime and Lauren. If you want, Mark and I can come over and we can have dinner and drinks. What do you say?"

"David, we have plans tonight, remember?"

"Ah shit. That's right. We're going to that party of that writer friend of yours."

"How about next weekend?" Mark asked.

"Sounds good to me," Sean said.

"Great!" They exclaimed.

Mark and David proceeded to kiss in front of Sean again. He turned the other way with a disgusted look on his face. He glanced back and noticed they were still kissing.

"Ugh. Get a room!"

Lunch Date

A week later, several buildings down and across the street in West Burnsville, Johnny and his friend, Ally Shay, was having lunch at the bistro, The Green Apple. The bistro was always a hit with the tourists and locals. Business is always booming no matter what time of year it is. With it being fall and the bistro being surrounded by the most beautiful scenery, it attracts a lot of attention. They're famous for their all-natural, all-organic home-style cuisine.

Johnny has been working as a server at The Green Apple since he moved to town five years ago. He met one of the owners at one of his gigs downtown. They struck up a conversation over a beer after the show. The owner discovered that Johnny was looking for more work to supplement his income, so he suggested he stop by his restaurant to see what he thought. A few days later, Johnny was his new server.

Ally, dressed in suit pants and a grey colored blouse, used to work at the bistro as a server. She worked there to put herself through school. Once she graduated, she got a job at a local design firm. She frequented the bistro often for lunch and to see her old friends and even talk to the owners who are like her mom and dad. Ally had never been close to her parents since they have not supported her decision to major in art instead of business. The owners had always supported her and have always been there for her no matter what. Even when she was having a difficult time paying her tuition junior year, they came through to help her and didn't even take it out of her pay.

Ally was very petite with ivory skin tone, blondish brown curly hair that she pulled back into a ponytail. She wore black-rimmed glasses, but they didn't disguise her beautiful brown eyes. She sat outside the bistro at one of the tables under a white pine. Johnny, wearing his server uniform, joined her for lunch before his shift started. The server brought them over menus and green teas. The servers and the cooks, like Johnny, are very attractive as well as artists. When you look at them, you see their attractiveness and beauty in the non-conventional sense. Their inner beauty, talent, and soul shine through. Their server was a painter who had a show last week that Ally attended. Ally was going to see if she can get the server a job at the firm.

"So, you all packed and ready to move?" Ally addressed Johnny.

"Yes. I'm moving in tomorrow!"

"How late are you working?"

"Till nine."

They both looked at the menu as if it has changed since the last time, they were there days prior. Ally put down the menu on the polished wooden table with matching chairs. "So how are things with you?"

Johnny shrugged, "Eh, pretty good considering."

"Considering?"

"Well, I got dumped a month ago. Other than that, I'm fucking fantastic!"

"No need to be a smartass! I was just asking how you were doing. I know it hurts and sucks, but you will get through this. It's just going to take some time to heal deep wounds."

Johnny drank his iced green tea. Ally drowned her tea with copious amounts of sugar while Johnny drank his straight.

"You know, it has gotten to the point where I don't wake up every morning wanting to hit something hard. I know that being pissed off at the world is getting old, but I've calmed down a lot. I have been doing Pilates and a lot more reading. I can now stop buying new alarm clocks since I smashed the last two, I've had."

Ally took a sip from her very sweet tea, "Well, I'm sure they would thank you if they could."

Johnny laughed and took another sip of his tea.

"So, I happened to notice you weren't at Midnights last night." Ally poured another packet of sugar in her tea.

"That would be correct!" Johnny said digging through his bookbag hanging on the chair behind him.

"Johnny…"

"Ally don't start! It's bad enough I must hear it from Seth constantly. I don't need to hear it from you, please!"

The server came back to the table to take their order. Johnny ordered a Reuben and soup while Ally ordered the turkey sandwich with sprouts and pasta salad. The server took the menus with a smile for both. Once the server left, Ally continued into Johnny, "You used to go to jam night at Midnights all the time. Seamus told me you have not been there in weeks."

"Seamus needs to mind his business and I'm sorry, but I don't feel like jamming right now! Having your heart kicked in will do that to you!"

"Johnny, this is not you. The 'Johnny' I know would not let a breakup get in between him and his music. I know its rough right now, but your music is who you are and you're not yourself these days. Do you think you need to go back to New York to get your head readjusted because if this is how you are going to be, maybe it would be good for you?"

Johnny looked off into the trees that surround the bistro. Ally tried to get his attention. "Hello"? Ally waved her hand in front of his face.

"New York is not the answer," Johnny responded. "I just need a little more time. You have no idea how much this hurts, Ally. When I was in love, I was so happy. That same happiness came through in my music. What's my music going to sound like now? No, New York is not the answer. I need to move on and forward here in Burnsville. This is my home now."

Ally reached across the table and put her hand on top of his. "You will get through this. You will find happiness again and it will again show through your music, different this time; better even! I'm here for you if you need me. You know that, right?"

"I know and thank you," Johnny sighed. "Remind me again why we stopped dating?"

Johnny and Ally used to be a hot item. They worked together and used to spend a lot of time with one another after work; playing pool, drinking beer, or just talking over cigarettes and coffee. Ally would go to every show of Johnny's band. At one of these shows, Ally met Seth. They developed a very strong friendship as well. They were like brothers and sisters. Ally introduced her friend, Kelly Northwood, to Seth a year ago. There was an instant attraction between them, and they've been dating ever since. Ally had a huge crush on Johnny months before them ever meeting but never said anything. She just told there in the distance admiring him at work, on stage blasting out a ballad or privately thinking naughty thoughts as he fingered his guitar.

One drunken night after they both pulled a double shift; they had gone back to Ally's place. After several bottles of wine, the sexual magnetism between them could no longer be contained. The morning after, they woke up and had sex two more times before finally taking a breath and decided to date each other. For a while, they were good together; inseparable. They spent most of their free time with one another and looked very happy until that temporary spark faded, and they decided they were both better off being friends.

Ally giggled. "I don't know. I had a crush on this cute, tough-looking New Yorker that rocked my world with his music, but then over time, I realized we were just better off as friends. I guess we got to know one another too much. It was nice while it lasted."

Johnny scoffed. "Nice?" Just nice?"

"What do you want me to say, that I saw fireworks, that you made my toes curl and the earth move?" Ally laughed.

"Well, it wouldn't hurt. It would help my bruised ego right now."

"Oh Johnny, you were the best. You made the earth move and my toes curl. You rocked my world. Oh baby, oh baby…better?" Ally said sarcastically.

"You're mean!" smiled Johnny.

"Ah, you know you love me."

"Funny, I don't think I'll ever be capable of loving someone again," Johnny said feeling sorry for himself.

"Not true. You will get back into your music. You will be inspired once more!"

At that moment, the server returned with their order and refilled their green tea. Ally immediately reached for the sugar. Johnny took the lemon from her glass knowing that she would not use it. Johnny drank his straight green tea with a lot of lemons. As he was squeezing the lemon into his tea, he noticed Sean walking down the sidewalk approaching them. He was wearing a long sleeve beige button-down shirt tucked into his brown dress slacks with a messenger bag across his chest. From the look of it, it was obvious that Sean was either going or coming from work. Johnny called out and waved at him. Sean noticed and waved back coming over to their table. When Sean got to the table, Johnny greeted him. "Sean! How are you, man?"

I'm good! I'm on a lunch break so decided to grab a bite to eat. I love this place!"

"Sean, this is my friend, Ally!"

Sean smiled at Ally shaking her hand. "Nice to meet you. I've heard a lot about you recently." Ally said.

"All good things I hope, Sean smiled, I'm sorry I won't keep you from lunch. I'm going to run in and get something myself."

"No, join us!" Johnny pulled the chair out, so Sean could sit. "What would you like? I can run in and get it for you."

"You don't have to do that."

"It's nothing. I work here. What would you like?"

"I'll have what you're having!"

"Good choice. I'll be right back. You want something to drink?"

"Green tea, extra lemon."

"Nice," smiled Johnny. He ran into the bistro to order Sean's food.

"So, are you excited about getting a new roomie?"

"Um, yes. Johnny seems cool."

"Yeah, he is. So, what do you do?"

"I go to school and work at the Burnsville Times."

"What are you studying?"

"Eh, that's still up in the air, but I'm leaning towards journalism," Sean replied. "And what about you? What do you do?"

"I'm a Graphic Designer at Xtreme-Art design firm down the street. Where are you going to school? UB?

"Yeah."

"That where I went…graduated two years ago."

"Oh cool."

He looked for Johnny with his food and drink. Ally noticed. "So, did you know that Johnny was a musician?"

Sean looked at Ally shocked, "No. I didn't know that."

"Well, I should say he used to be a musician. He stopped playing some weeks ago. He's so freaking talented."

"Really?" Sean smiled. "Um, why did he stop playing?"

"He got his heartbroken. It messed him up."

"I can relate to that. Just got dumped actually," Sean said softly.

"I guess you guys have something in common."

Sean smirked, "We do. Well, I'm guessing there might be some differences with our breakups and relationships.

"Breakups are breakups. Love is love. There is nothing different about that. They happen, and they end. That's it!"

"Oh, believe me. There are some differences."

Ally looked confused but brushed it off when she saw Johnny approaching with Sean's food and drink. He set it down in front of Sean and looked at them.

"So, what did I miss?"

They both answers, "Nothing."

Sean took a big gulp from his tea; Ally did the same thing and Johnny just stood there feeling very left out.

Moving Day

Thursday had finally arrived, and Sean waited for Johnny to move in. He sat in his living room with Michele. Michelle was very tall, about 6-foot-tall, short dark hair and thin. She moved to Burnsville from Massachusetts during her first year. She was taller than the average woman and gorgeous. Not only was she intelligent but had the body and looks that could very well get her a modeling contract tomorrow. She was extremely down to earth and loved her coffee and cell phone. If you were to catch her on the street, she would have a coffee in one hand and her phone glued to her ear. She worked part-time at an art gallery as an assistant to the gallery manager. Something that started as just an afternoon internship for school turned into a great paying opportunity and experience. The gallery was in West Burnsville, the same one where the server from The Green Apple had her show last week. She hoped to run a gallery one day. Her major was art history with a minor in journalism. If the gallery manager doesn't work out, she would like to write art reviews for a paper or magazine in Europe.

Michelle, wearing a pair of tight jeans with holes in them and a white Hanes t-shirt, came out of the kitchen with two cups of tea. She handed one to Sean, who was sitting on the mutilated recliner now covered with a comforter and took her cup and sat on the couch. "Well, let me just say that I don't blame you for getting a roommate. I think it is a great idea."

"Yeah, maybe it's for the best." Sean agreed.

Michele sipped her tea, "Ugh, I never liked Jaime anyway."

Sean was about to sip his tea then stopped, "What is this, truth month?!"

"Sorry but couldn't tell you that before. You were so happy and in love."

"I'm so glad to see happiness and love outweighs honesty among my friends and family," Sean sipped his tea.

"Well, I think Dave might be right. Maybe you should put yourself out there. Go on a date. Put a personal ad in the paper. Get your mind off all of this."

"I know you'll are right, but I just wish there was something I could've done to prevent Jaime from leaving. If so, then I wouldn't be contemplating going on dates or putting a personal ad in the paper."

"Okay, first, you need to stop thinking you're the reason this relationship is over. It's getting really old."

"Everyone seems to agree with you."

"That's because we're right and you need to listen to us!"

The doorbell rang. Sean put down his cup and got up from the recliner. "That must be Johnny. Are you going to stick around?

"Nah, I think I'm going to head out and get some homework done," Michele got up and set her cup on the coffee table. "Call me later. Let's go to Midnights and get a drink!"

"Great."

Sean and Michelle walked to the door. Sean opened the door and was greeted by Johnny, wearing a white tank top and jeans, holding a box with Seth behind him holding an even bigger box. Sean and Michelle couldn't help but notice Johnny's arm muscles slightly flexed and numerous tattoos. Michelle kissed Sean on the cheek and moved past Johnny and Seth. "Hey there, guys."

Michelle walked down the hallway as Seth stared leaving his lower jaw and tongue on the floor. Johnny couldn't help but look at the very statuesque Michelle left their sight.

Seth whistled, "Damn, she is fine!"

Johnny rolled his eyes and grinned at Sean. "Easy there, boy."

"Here, let me help you." Sean laughed as he took the box from Johnny.

"Thanks, man."

They both entered the apartment as Sean set the box on the floor in the living room. "Do you have a lot of stuff to move in?" Sean asked Johnny.

"Just a few more boxes and my television. I'm going to have to make an extra trip to get all of my clothes." Seth set the box down on the couch as he looked around the apartment. "Yes, out of MY apartment! Whoa. This place is nice."

"Oh man, I'm sorry. Sean, this is my best friend, Seth."

Sean shook Seth's hand, "Hey."

"Heard about your last roommate moving out suddenly," Seth asked quizzically.

"Seth!"

"What? I'm just saying must be expensive to pay for all this alone."

"What the...?" Johnny uttered.

Sean laughed, "It's cool. I got this place with my ex, not a roommate. We broke up."

"Oh. Did she have money or something?" Seth inquired.

"Seth!"

"What?!"

"Sean, I apologize for my friend's rudeness. He forgets his manners when he meets someone new; especially if they're not wearing a skirt."

"It's okay," Sean laughed. "I work and make pretty good money. It's just not good enough to live here by myself. The extra person does help. So, I guess I'll let you get settled in and if you need anything, my room is right down the hall." Sean walked down the hallway to his room and closed the door behind him. Johnny looked at Seth and punched him in his arm.

"Ouch! What was that for?"

"What's with the questions?!"

"I was curious…"

"This is *not* the first date. He's a roommate. Not some girl I'm introducing to my parents…. Dad!"

"Hey, I was just making sure he wasn't crazy or psychotic."

"Well, at least that answers the question of how he might see YOU!"

"Funny. Well, let's go back to get the rest of your stuff."

"I'm going to stay here and unpack. Here, takes the keycard so you can get back in."

Johnny handed the card to Seth from his back pocket. Seth left the apartment and Johnny opened one of the boxes on the floor. As he was walking down the hallway, Seth let out a monster belch. Johnny began to laugh.

"Classy."

Johnny unpacked some beer mugs from the box. He got up and walked them over to the kitchen. After setting them on the counter, he walked back into the living room. He noticed the answering machine light blinking with one message. Sean came out of his bedroom and noticed Johnny walking back to unpack the rest of the box on the floor. Sean looked around and noticed Seth wasn't around.

"Hey, where's your friend?" Sean asked.

"He went to get some more boxes from the apartment. You have a message on the machine."

Sean looks over to the answering machine and walks over to the table. "That's funny, I didn't even hear the phone ring."

Sean hit the play button. The message that played was from Jaime, a message he didn't intend on Johnny hearing.

You have one saved message. First saved message…… (Beep)…. (Male voice) Sean, we need to talk. Listen, I know you're upset, but you need to get over it. You and I are finished! I've moved on. Why don't you do yourself a favor and do the same. Don't be mad at Lauren. This is not her fault. Later…… (Beep).

Sean stood there staring at the machine. "Fuck," he said under his breath.

Johnny stops unpacking and looked at Sean, "I take it that was your ex?"

"Yes…Jaime," Sean uncomfortably said.

"So, your ex was a guy?"

"Yes."

"You're gay…"

"Yes, I am. Listen, if you want to change your mind about living here now that you know…"

Johnny stood up. "Whoa, man. Relax. I have no issue with you being gay. You could've told me that you were gay, and it wouldn't make a difference in me moving in here with you. You seem like a cool guy. That is what matters."

Sean smiled, "Thanks." Sean walked over and sat on the comforter-covered recliner. Johnny walked back and sat on the floor next to the box he was unpacking. Johnny continued to pull his possessions out of the box and noticed Sean looking out the window.

"So, if you don't mind me asking, what happened between you two?"

Sean sighed. "He dumped me."

"I'm sorry." Johnny stopped unpacking.

"We were together for a year. I met him at the college bookstore and thought he was so cute. I couldn't take my eyes off him. We made eyes at one another from opposite book aisles before I got the nerve to walk over to the aisle where he was pretending to look for a book. We talked, I invited him for coffee, and then coffee turned to dinner. It was like magic. It was my first relationship with a man. Hell, my first relationship with anyone. I'd never felt the way Jaime made me feel in the beginning. I thought I was in heaven, walking on cloud nine all the time".

Sean sighed, "Well, six months after we started dating, we moved in here together. Everything seemed fine. There were some rough patches, but nothing that could not be fixed and worked out. He was worth it. He made my world complete. I loved him with all my heart. Who knew it would all end just as soon as it began?"

"Damn."

"Oh, it gets worse. The guy he's with now, he had been seeing four months before we broke up. They moved in with one another soon after."

"Do you know who this other guy is?"

"No. I don't think I want to either."

"His loss, man."

"Thanks", Sean said softly and then cleared his throat, "So what about you? Girlfriend?

Johnny got up off the floor and sat on the couch across from Sean in the recliner. "Well, my friend, I think you and I share the same heartache, but my girlfriend didn't dump me. She cheated on me, with some guy in our shower."

"In love with cheaters. Who knew?" Sean grinned.

"Two months ago, I came home from work to surprise her with a proposal. We had been together for three years and I thought she was the one. Natalie, that's her name, and I shared an apartment and I was working extra shifts at the bistro to put a down payment on a house. When I came home, the shower was on in the bedroom. I thought I would surprise her and get in with her until I realized as I got closer to the bathroom she was not alone. I think the moans and stepping over clothes that were not mine were a dead giveaway. I could smell his cologne…everywhere. The smell, damn, that smell I will never get out of my nose. I grabbed some stuff, threw the ring on the bed, and never came back. I called her cell hours later and left a message on her voicemail that it was over and that I hope she enjoyed the shower.

"Wow. I'm sorry, man, but if I were you, I would've kept the ring."

"There was no point. It meant nothing anymore. All that it did represent was gone."

Sean leaned forward in the recliner, "Did you ever think about working it out?"

"A second chance?"

"Yes."

"No. I don't give second chances when someone cheats on me. When I'm with someone, I'm just with that person and that person only. There should be no reason or need to cheat."

"You should tell Jaime that."

"Only if you tell Natalie first."

They both laughed.

"We experienced love's kick in the ass. I think a friendship might come out of it." Johnny noted.

"You know, I think you're right! To hell with them! We shall find two people with good hearts that will not cheat and treat us just as good as we treat them!"

"Here, here!"

"And we will love even harder and better than before!"

"Now that's something I do best...love!"

"Same here, my friend!"

They looked at one another with slight intensity behind their eyes. Sean got out of the recliner and sat on the floor, "The other day, Ally mentioned you were a musician. Is that true?"

"Yeah, it's true. I *was* a musician."

"Was...?"

"I think my passion...my inspiration for music died with my relationship with Natalie."

"Getting your heart broken can diminish your passion."

"It's tough, but I'm making some progress."

"Do you think you'll ever be inspired again? Create music with passion behind it?"

"Raise it from the dead? I don't know..."

"Well, I would like to feel that passion one day," Sean smiled.

Johnny smirked, "Maybe you will," he added softly.

"I hope so," Sean replied still smiling.

The doorbell rang. Sean got up off the floor and answered the door. He thought Seth had returned with more boxes, but when he opened the door, he was shocked to see Jaime standing there in a red cashmere V-neck sweater with a pink undershirt, grey slacks, and Gucci shoes twirling a key on his finger. "I'm returning the key."

Jaime was in his early twenties, five feet eleven inches, good looking, very tan from platinum membership at the tanning salon. He looks like money and always dresses like it. He looks down on those who don't have it or looks it and flaunts his platinum and gold cards every chance he gets. If Jaime has money, it's not from his hard work ethic, but more his father's very generous allowance; which you would think was odd still receiving an allowance over the age of 21. If he could have his way, Jaime would continue getting that allowance until the bank went dry.

He attended the University of Burnsville's very competitive business program. He drove a shiny black BMW with leather interior and chrome rims on the tires. He spends more time and money at the tanning bed, mall, or beach than class. He had a dark sense of humor and smart but was very conceited when it came to his personality. He was charming and liked by a select few, but their people out there that would think and say differently.

Sean left Jaime standing in the doorway still twirling the key.

"You should've mailed it."

Jaime walked into the apartment and checked out the place. Sean walked over to the kitchen while Johnny was still on the couch in the living room.

Jaime noticed Johnny, "Well, you know I would've mailed it, but I heard you had someone moving in today. So, I figured I'd bring the key over personally and meet the loser who decided to live with you."

"I think I would be that loser you're referring to." Johnny repositioned himself on the couch.

Jaime smiled at him, "I wouldn't want your new roomie here to think I was an asshole or anything," addressing Sean in the kitchen.

"Well, keep up the good work!" Sean quipped sarcastically. "Johnny, this is Jaime."

Jaime glared at Johnny with a smirk on his face, "Ah, Johnny, the pleasure is all yours. I don't know if Sean has told you, but we used to date."

"I might have heard that," Johnny said coldly.

"Did he tell you that I was the love of his life?" Jaime giggled. "Yeah, well, don't worry. The feelings weren't mutual."

"Why would I worry?" Johnny asked.

"Well, for Sean to get someone as hot as you to move in here with him, there must be something more going on here than just splitting the utilities," Jaime grinned.

Johnny stood up from the couch, "Look, Sean and I are just roommates and that's all, so if you're implying that we're more than just that, then you're sadly mistaken."

Jaime found himself suddenly face to face with Johnny. Sean came out from the kitchen and stood behind the recliner.

"You need to back up," Johnny warned.

"Aren't we touchy? You better watch out, Sean, these straight boys don't take to kind to us homosexuals coming on to them."

"I'm not like you, Jaime. You're the only one here acting like a fag!"

Jaime backed up and started laughing at Sean who looked very uncomfortable standing behind the recliner, "Geez, I was only kidding with him. Where's your sense of humor? Damn, I keep forgetting you're such a lame-ass."

Johnny took a deep breath while clenching his fists but then exhaled as he relaxed them. He then walked over to the very uncomfortable Sean who was shaking a little at this point. "Listen, Jaime, you dropped off the key and had some laughs at Sean's expense. Why don't you just get out of here and leave him alone!"

Jaime stood there looking at them with one hand on his hip, "How sweet." He then walked over to them both standing behind the recliner, "Listen…Johnny…my name is still on the lease! I can stand here and say whatever I want."

"Then you should be paying half the rent and utilities!" Johnny snapped.

Jaime scoffed, "Why would I do that? I don't live here with this loser…you do!" Jaime poked at Johnny's chest. "You take care of it!" Johnny smacked Jaime's hand away and lunged for him. Sean stopped him by grabbing him and praying to God the recliner was in the way of giving Jaime the beating of his life. "Johnny, Johnny! Could I have a moment alone with Jaime? Please? It's cool. It's cool. It'll be okay."

Johnny calmed down for the moment, "Sure, no problem. I'm going to have a smoke. I'll be right outside if you need me."

"Thanks."

Johnny cautiously walked by Jaime who continued to glare at him with a grin. Johnny walked to the front door of the apartment. Jaime still holding the key to the apartment, "Wait! You might need this to get back in, sweet Johnny."

Johnny turned back and snatched the key from Jaime. This time he had a little message for him that he whispered in his ear, *"Better watch your ass. If you fuck with him again, you will have to deal with me, and I don't kiss nice."*

"Don't tease me," Jaime moaned. "Is that a threat?"

"It's a guarantee!" Johnny grinned and bit his lower lip trying to hold back every urge to slug him. He then looked at Sean standing near the recliner before walking towards the door. He opened the door to leave and as he was about to close it behind him, Jaime had a little message for him, "See you soon…. lover. I mean, Johnny." Jaime smirked.

Johnny hesitated, and then closed the door behind him. He stood there for a moment sensing something familiar yet strange, but then shrugged it off and continued outside to have a cigarette. He ran into Seth in the hallway.

"Hey. Where are you going? I got your stuff," Seth said to Johnny.

"Um, I need some air. It's best if we don't go in there right now. Come on."

"What's going on?"

"I'll explain it to you outside. Come on!" Johnny grabbed Seth by the arm as he directed him down the hallway explaining what had happened in the apartment.

"He's such a sweetheart," Jaime sarcastically asked Sean about Johnny.

"No. You're such an asshole!" He replied.

"Ah, yes, this is true."

"You dropped off the key, insulted my roommate, and sweet-talked me. Anything else you would like to add?"

Jaime walked over to the couch, sat down, and puts his feet up on the coffee table, "How about you and I have a little chat?" Jaime patted the seat cushion next to him. Sean was hesitant at first, but then moved over slowly to the couch and sat next to Jaime. Jaime turned slightly to Sean who was sitting up looking straight ahead, "Sean, look at me," Jaime said softly. Sean turned to Jaime slowly. Jaime met Sean's watery eyes with a smile. "You know, I talked to Lauren."

"I was wondering how you knew about Johnny. She can keep her mouth shut about certain things yet open it about others."

Jaime moved closer, "Hey, I think it's great you are getting someone else to move in with you. I mean, don't you think it's about time we all move on and forward with our lives? Hell, I know I have!"

Sean looked at Jaime with lost in his eyes. Jaime responded by gently touching the side of Sean's face, "The memory of me still lingers in your eyes and face. I see that clear as day and it's oh so very sad."

"It's only been a month. How could you move on so fast? Didn't I mean anything to you? Didn't you care?" Sean said with a little sadness behind his voice.

"Oh, sweetie...." Jaime paused with empathy and puts his hand on Sean's knee. Sean put his hand on top of Jaime's hand and gave it a little squeeze, "I found someone better than you." He removed Sean's hand, got up, and walked over to the other side of the room noticing some art pieces on the floor leaning against the wall. Sean sat there somewhat shock after being sweet-talked by Jaime.

"Yuck. You've always had such lousy taste," he remarked about the artwork.

"I dated you, didn't I?" Sean replied.

"What did you say?"

Sean cleared his throat, "Those are Johnny's."

"That figures."

"I think it's time for you to go now."

Jaime turned and walked back over to Sean still sitting on the couch. He stood looking down at him as Sean's head was in his lap, "Oh, don't sit there looking so heartbroken. It's for the best it happened this way. You'll see. One day you will find someone just as inadequate as you. I was never that person! I mean, look at me! You were never good enough for me. No matter how much you tried to love me, it didn't matter, because I was never in love with you. I think I felt sorry for you more than anything." Jaime sighed and began to walk towards the front door to leave. Sean dropped his head in between his knees and sobbed. He turned back to Sean, "See, look at you! You're sitting here sobbing and looking a wreck over someone who couldn't stand to be with your ass…pathetic!" Jaime reached for his keys in his pocket and opened the door, "Next time, don't be so quick to fall for someone you meet in the campus bookstore."

Sean sobbed, "For a year, I gave you all that was in my heart to give. For a year, I was devoted to no one else but you and for a year, you didn't love me at all?

Jaime chuckled, "Like I said, pathetic." Jaime closed the door behind him leaving Sean sobbing in the living room. He fell to the floor and curled up in a ball between the couch and coffee table. Johnny and Seth returned to the apartment with more boxes moments and noticed Sean on the floor crying. Johnny put down the box on the floor and ran to Sean.

"Sean! Are you okay? What's wrong?" Johnny put his hand on his back trying to supply some sort of comfort to him.

"I'm okay, leave me alone. Please," Sean cried out from between his knees.

Seth stood there holding a box watching Johnny trying to console Sean. Johnny got up, walked around the coffee table, and picked up the box from the floor. Johnny looked at Seth and motioned to go back to his bedroom. A few minutes later, Sean was still sobbing. Johnny poked his head out of his room still able to see Sean on the floor. He wanted to say something and comfort him at that moment but couldn't. He went back into his room, not saying a word.

To Know You

The next day, Johnny came home to find Sean cooking in the kitchen. That was something new to see. Natalie or Seth didn't cook, but Johnny made many meals for him and Natalie when they were together. Johnny used to cook all the time when he lived in New York. Something he learned from his father. His father cooked a lot for him and his brothers growing up. Even though his father full time, he would still come home and cook a nice, healthy meal for the boys. If it wasn't hamburgers or spaghetti or stir fry, it was a big healthy salad. Johnny's mother worked a lot and mostly cooked breakfast and dinner on the weekends. She was also in charge of cooking the holiday meals that would usually take two days to prepare. He can remember coming home around Thanksgiving time and just smelling the aromas of sweet potato pies, dressing and macaroni, and cheese in the air. Walking in that door brought back some great memories of home.

Johnny dropped his shoes and skateboard by the door. He drifted towards the kitchen where the delicious aromas illuminated. Johnny stopped at the dining room table and set down his keys and wallet.

"Johnny?"

"Man, whatever you're cooking smells amazing!"

"It's dinner! I hope you're hungry."

Johnny walked into the kitchen and noticed Sean making a salad. He also noticed fresh rolls on the counter, several pots on the stove simmering, which was where most of the aroma was coming from and something baking in the oven.

"Wow. It smells amazing in here. I didn't know you were such a good cook."

Sean laughed, "Well, taste the food first before you make that assumption."

Johnny walked over to the stove and Sean followed. Sean stirred one of the pots and puts a little sauce on a spoon allowing Johnny to taste. He blew on it and fed it to Johnny. After Johnny had a taste, he looked as if he was going to faint.

"Good?" Sean asked.

"That's so good…spicy!"

Johnny sat down at the kitchen table as Sean showed him what he has been doing most of the evening. "Well, I hope you like enchiladas because that is what's cooking in the oven. I also made a salad, got some cold beer in the fridge, fresh rolls over there, and my famous beans and rice!"

"Great! I can't wait. You know, I could get use to this!" Johnny changed the subject clearing his throat. "Sean, I wanted to talk to you about last night…"

Sean continued fixing the salad at the counter near the sink. "Um, I don't want to talk about it, okay?"

"I know it's hard, but if you…."

Sean stopped with the salad and turned to Johnny. "I don't want to talk about it. Please talk about something else."

Johnny got up and pushed the chair under the table. "Cool. I'm going to take a shower and get ready for dinner."

Sean stood there in silence looking down at the counter and the salad fixings. As Johnny left the kitchen, he took off his shirt. Sean stepped over to the doorway and watched as Johnny walked down the hallway to the bathroom wearing nothing but jeans. Sean noticed his back and shoulder muscles move as he swaggered down the hall. He also noticed Johnny's butt move in his loose jeans with holes in the back pockets with his boxer briefs exposed above the belt time of his jeans.

Johnny went into his room, the room that was the office across from Sean's bedroom, instead of the bathroom. Sean couldn't help but fantasized for a moment about Johnny as he walked down the hallway, playing in slow motion in his mind. Johnny came back out of his room, now just wearing boxer briefs, and went into the bathroom. As he stood there, his eyes opened wider and his mouth watered with lust, he came out of the trance when he finally heard the shower running. He couldn't help but imagine who would want to shower with anyone else but Johnny. He went back to the counter and finished the salad. He grabbed a kitchen towel and wiped the perspiration off his forehead.

A few days later, Sean was walking to the record store downtown. Before he walked into Daddy Pimp's Record Store, Sean reached in his book bag and grabbed his wallet. He opened the door and noticed Johnny skateboarding towards him. Johnny had his shades on, cigarette hanging from his lip, baggy pants, vintage tee with Rolling Stones logo, and a corduroy jacket. As Johnny approached, Sean's heartbeat started pounding in his chest. Johnny hopped off the board and took off his shades.

"Hey. Where you headed?" Sean asked coyly.

Johnny laughs, "Um, here actually."

Sean stood there chuckling uncomfortably blocking the doorway.

"Are you going?" Johnny grinned.

Sean let Johnny in and followed. Johnny walked down the aisle looking at records on one side while Sean looked on the other side.

"You into vinyl?"

"Oh yes. I have a record player in my room. It was a gift……from Jaime. I think it was the nicest thing he had ever given me or did for me."

Johnny laughed, "That says a lot. So, what kind of music are you into?"

"Classic rock…Alternative…80's stuff... How about you?"

"Huh, you and Ally should get along then. She loves that stuff. I like more early punk and rap."

"Nice."

Sean moved to the other aisle opposite Johnny. He admired Johnny as he looked at the records. Johnny caught him a few times looking at him across the aisle but continued to flip through the records.

"See anything you like?" Johnny smiled still flipping through the records.

"Oh yes..." Sean stared at Johnny.

Johnny looked up from the records, "Really, what did you find?"

Busted, Sean quickly looked down at the records. He noticed Sean startled and grins. Sean frantically picked up the first record he could get his hands on without looking at it. Johnny reached across and grabbed the record out of his hand. Puzzled, Johnny showed Sean the record he so carelessly chose.

"Amy Grant? This is something good you found?"

Sean's voice trembled, "She had some good songs."

Johnny stared at him as if he has lost his mind. "I'm sorry but you just don't seem like the Amy Grant type."

"Hey, there are a lot of things about me that you don't know. Some would surprise you….and you should not judge a book by its cover. I thought someone like you would know and realize that… being an artist!"

Johnny laughed, "Why are you getting so defensive?"

"I'm not getting defensive. I'm just saying…."

"You're saying don't judge an Amy Grant fan by its cover?!"

Sean reached across and snatched the album back from Johnny. "Oh, shut up. This is a good album," shaking the album at Johnny.

Sean walked over to the cashier. Johnny stood there laughing to himself. He continued to look through the records, found a Led Zeppelin album he's always wanted, went up to the counter and stood behind Sean. There were two other customers ahead of Sean in line.

"So, did you find anything else you liked?" Johnny asked playfully.

Sean rolled his eyes, "Nope. This was it. Nothing else that I saw interests me."

"Really? That's interesting because I thought I noticed you looking at something else."

Sean closed his eyes and exhaled, "Ahem. Nope. Not a thing. Ahem. Did you find anything you liked?"

"Oh yes. I found Led Zeppelin III."

Sean turned halfway towards Johnny a little surprised. "That's my favorite album."

Johnny still playful, "Is it now?"

Sean turned completely to Johnny, "Yes. My friends and I used to play that album all the time when we'd come home from school. Only one of us had the album so we would take turns listening to it at each other's house."

"Maybe I'll let you borrow mine sometime."

Sean laughed, "I own it."

"Imagine that."

Sean smiled and turned back around in line. There was only one person ahead of him in line. Johnny decided to have a little fun with Sean. "You know, I listened to an Amy Grant song once. Natalie used to love the song, *Baby, Baby*. She would play it throughout the apartment all the time." Johnny giggled and moved so close to Sean to where his mouth was barely touching the back of his neck and ear lobe. Sean closed his eyes and licked his lips as he felt Johnny's breath on the back of his neck. "She would dance around me in her underwear to that damn song. I admit I got excited seeing her body move to that song. Wait, maybe it was just the song that got me so hot. Do you know that song, Sean? Did it get you hot, too?"

Sean mumbled with his eyes still closed, "Yeah, I guess...a little."

Trying not to giggle, Johnny moved in just a little closer where his lips were touching the little hairs on Sean's ear. It was not the Amy Grant song that was making Sean hot at this very moment. Johnny got back into character, "Yeah, you know that song or yes, that it gets you hot? It doesn't matter. I just know that I was so horny and had to satisfy my 'excitement' if you know what I mean. I needed sex right then. I was completely throbbing in my pants. It just needed to be unzipped and touched. You know, stroke my ego a little bit. Mm, can you imagine that?"

"Yes. Yes. I can imagine. Oh God, yes!" Sean whispered.

Sean was completely hypnotized by Johnny's words, his voice and his smell of Irish Spring mixed with sweat got him drunk with excitement. He started to perspire and leaned his head back a little bit. The cashier got Sean's attention since he was next in line and holding up the other customers. Johnny did everything he could to hold back his laughter.

"Excuse me, sir?" The cashier said.

Sean opened his eyes and finally heard the cashier. He wiped his forehead and straightened up. The cashier signals for the album so he can complete the purchase. Sean moved up and hands it to him. Johnny could no longer contain himself and exploded with laughter. Sean, embarrassed, turned to him. "What's so funny?!"

"Dude, it's okay if you were checking me out."

"What??!"

"I noticed you checking me out," Johnny still laughing. "It's no big deal. It happens all the time. I can't help it if some find me irresistible and delicious."

"Delicious? Really? Sean was embarrassed but tried to save face. "I see we're a little full of ourselves."

Johnny shrugged, "Not at all. Just saying it has happened before and it's not a big deal to me. So, I figured I would fuck with you."

Sean turned back to the cashier, grabbed his change and album.

"Well, I wasn't checking you out," Sean said defensively. "So, rest assure that I will not become part of a fan club that thinks you're God's gift!"

He started to walk away. Johnny gave his album to the cashier, "Sean!"

Sean turned around, "What?"

"You have a little drool on your chin," Johnny smirked.

Sean checked his chin and realized that Johnny was messing with him again, "Asshole." He turned and stormed out of the shop. Johnny gave his credit card to the cashier but still couldn't resist laughing at Sean; neither could the cashier.

Midnights

The next day at school, Sean and his friend Craig were leaving their Modern Literature class. Sean and Craig had been friends since their first year. Craig was on the swimming team and played soccer for the university. Craig was known as one of the popular guys on campus. He was well-liked by his peers as well as professors alike. He was very nice and charming and considered an intellectual. He was Sean's height, slightly bigger athletic build, had long dirty blond hair and green eyes that shined like emeralds. Sean slung his messenger bag across his chest and Craig carried his books under his arm. Craig always wore flip flops no matter what the weather was like outside. Sean noticed he wore sneakers once when there was snow on the ground. Other than that, you could expect to see Craig in jeans or shorts, some sort of logo tee, and flip flops. Today, Craig didn't vary from his wardrobe except for an Old Navy scarf around his neck.

"So, what are you doing tonight?" Craig asked Sean as they walked down the hallway.

"I'm going to The Open Hats concert with Johnny."

"No shit...where are they playing?"

"At Burns Theater in West Burnsville," Sean said as they took the stairwell to the first floor. "What are you doing tonight?"

"I've got a date with this girl from my History of Film class. Then we're going to a party some guy from the swimming team is throwing. You guys should stop by!"

"I'm not sure if the jock party scene is really Johnny's thing and you know damn well it isn't mine!" Sean smiled.

"You might have a good time, though. I know it's been tough for you lately. It might be good to get out there and get completely shit faced!"

"Well, my cousin will be taking care of that tomorrow night. We're all going out to Midnights for drinks. Are you coming?

"Going to Boston for the weekend with the parents but have some shots for me!" Craig opened the door to leave the building. They walked out to the courtyard in the direction of the student parking lot. Craig stopped Sean, "Hey, I know I haven't been around that much lately, but are you sure you're okay?"

"Yeah, I mean, it was tough in the beginning, but I'm doing okay. I'm glad Johnny moved in. It's nice to have someone else there in the apartment...especially helping with the bills, but it's nice to have someone else there to talk to...you know?"

"Yeah, and you guys seemed to have hit it off!"

"He's a good guy. He's going through the same shit as me, so we can relate on that level."

"That's good." Craig sighed. "Just glad I haven't seen Jaime around campus lately! If I did, I'd probably beat the shit out of him!"

"Well, you would have to get in line, and let me tell you that line is very long!"

Craig patted Sean on his shoulder as they went ahead to the parking lot. "Well, I'm glad to see some of that asshole's effect on you is wearing off..."

"Yeah..." Sean smiled.

Craig walked off to his car and Sean walked off in the other direction. Sean didn't realize how far he had parked from campus. Parking on campus has become a complete nightmare and seems to just be getting worst year after year. If you're not on campus by dawn, you are guaranteed not to get a spot close to campus, so best advised to bring your walking shoes.

Sean sighed with some relief, thinking about the hold that Jaime had on him was wearing very thin. No personal ad was necessary. Just a good friend who happen to also be a good roommate, but he could help but wonder if someone's effect was developing a hold on him in a good way, but this good way could also be a bad one; especially to those who don't feel the same way.

It was Friday night and the place to be was Midnights. Guys in suits, women in dresses and heels mixed with college students dressed in jeans and tees with the occasional shorts with tank tops. There was no band that night, but with energy in the lounge, it wasn't necessary. The jukebox was playing, and the drinks were flowing. The conversation volume was low enough to where you could hear the music, hear the person or persons across from you and order a drink from the bartender without losing your voice. There were a few patrons on the small dance floor enjoying the music and seemed to have some sense of rhythm. The ones that didn't want to look silly so early in the evening stood on the sides of the floor swaying from side to side with drinks in their hand building up the courage to express their rhythm-less nation.

Johnny sat at the bar talking to the bartender, Seamus, a native of Dublin moved to the States when he was seventeen. He lived in New York for several years before moving to Burnsville. Sean and Lauren spent most of the night avoiding one another and making eyes at each other from across the bar. Sean was sitting with Michelle, who was worried about Sean since he was drinking a little more than usual that night. David and Mark were at the bar talking to the other bartender working that night, Chris, who went to high school with David. Seth and Kelly were at a cozy table in the corner having a few drinks and enjoying each other's company.

Chris the bartender looked across the bar and noticed Sean, "So how's your cousin doing?" he asked handing David a beer.

David turned to look in the direction where Sean and Michelle were seated, "He's doing okay. Jaime stopped by the other night and it upset him. I'm just glad he decided to come out tonight."

Mark turned and noticed Sean laughing and talking very loudly, "Yeah, by the looks of it, he's feeling no pain, but what I don't understand is why Jaime is bothering himself with Sean? I mean, he dumped him, why doesn't he just leave him alone?"

"Maybe he gets off on seeing Sean upset and miserable," Chris said.

David took a swig of his beer, "I think you may be right. I also feel that Sean thinks he still needs Jaime, which is not true. He feels lost without him, that he's incomplete. I mean, we've been there, with whomever we were with; we have that need inside to belong to someone. He just needs to find that one guy that will need him as much as them…show him what true love is. Jaime was never right for Sean."

"Yeah, Jaime was never capable of that. He's too selfish and the only thing he got from Jaime was headache and heartache." Mark said.

"Yes!" David agreed.

Sean, wearing a black button-down shirt with jeans with Michelle dressed in a maroon sequenced dress that was slit up the side with furry high heel boots. She had a purple feathered shawl across her shoulders. Sean chased down a shot and followed it with a shot.

"Sean, don't you think you should slow down?" Michelle noticed.

"You're right!"

The server happened to past the table at that time. Sean, tapping her arm, orders another drink and shot, "Excuse me, may I get vodka and Red Bull and only ONE shot this time?"

"Sure!" The server said as she turned to go back to the bar. Standing next to Johnny, she orders the drink and shot from Seamus. Johnny looked at Sean.

"Thank you!"

"That is not what I meant." Michelle sighed.

"Hey, what's the problem? It's a happy hour…and I'm happy and not obsessing over my asshole of an ex-boyfriend. Isn't that what everyone wants?!"

"Yes, but not by drowning yourself in vodka and shots!"

"Well, trust me, it's working quite nicely!" Sean said with a slur behind his words.

Michelle stared at Sean, "You know, Johnny told me that Jaime came by the apartment. He also told me that you were very upset when he left, which is why I think you're drinking the way you are tonight. Am I right?" Michelle paused for a reaction from Sean, but he just ignored her statement, "What did he do?" she asked.

"He did what Jaime always does…be Jaime."

The server returned from Sean's drink and shot. Sean looked over at the bar at Johnny looking at him. Seamus poured Johnny another shot of whiskey which took his attention of Sean. "So, are you back on the market?" Seamus asked pushing the shot in front of Johnny.

Johnny picked up the shot and downed it, "I'm going to enjoy being single for a long time, my friend. Love is bullshit."

"I know you don't believe that." Seamus took a shot of whiskey as well and took away the shot glasses, "I'm getting you another beer."

"It's too much trouble…causes too much pain."

"I don't think that's love, I think that's the person whom you choose to love," Seamus said pouring Johnny another beer.

"You don't choose to love someone. It just happens. You have no control over who you fall in love with. Such a deadly emotion."

Johnny and Seamus met several years ago when Johnny's band began performing at Midnights. Seamus convinced his bar manager to make the band a house band. They would play every Friday night for a set fee depending on the crowd. The more the people who attended their show, the increase in bar sales and the more money the band made. Johnny was appreciative of Seamus for the connection and the extra cash. When the bar manager was fired, the contract mysteriously disappeared under new management and the band started just performing once a month, which hurt their huge following, but the fans who were truly loyal never missed a show.

Seamus walked over to Johnny with a pint, "So, when are you going to get back to your music?"

"Talking to Seth again, I see," Johnny uttered.

"It was Ally. She's worried about you, you know."

"I don't want to talk about it."

"Okay, you don't want to talk about it." Seamus changed the subject. "So, how's the roommate thing working out?"

"It's cool. Sean's a nice guy, but I feel bad for the guy having to go through that shit with his ex. Man, let me tell you, he's a real dick!"

"Oh really?"

"Yeah, first, the guy stopped by the apartment to return the key. He did nothing but talk shit about Sean… and me! The fucker doesn't even know me! I wanted to punch him in his fucking mouth, but I didn't let my temper get the best of me this time. I think it got to Sean more than it did me. I came back to the apartment. The douche was gone, Sean on the floor crying. It was messed up."

"Damn…well, some situations with ex-lovers are tougher than others," Seamus poured himself and Johnny another shot, "Just be there for the man if you can because it sounds like he's going to need a lot of friends in his corner right now."

Johnny pondered after downing the shot, "You know what, there's something about this ex of his, Jaime. I don't know exactly what it is, but it's like I've met him before or seen him before, but not in a memorable way."

"Maybe you met him at a show?"

"I don't think so. He just seems too preppy and bitchy. I've always wondered what Sean saw in that guy. It makes you wonder what attracts one person to another, doesn't it?"

Seamus grinned, "Yeah makes you wonder." Seamus felt something more was going on in Johnny's mind and he had to question it, "You seem to have gotten pretty close to this guy in such a short amount of time. What's with that?"

Seamus waited for an answer from Johnny as he turned away from Seamus to avoid making eye contact. He finished his pint and Seamus, sensing avoidance, walked away to tend to the other patrons at the end of the bar. Johnny looked over at Seth and Kelly and noticed Seth looking back at him.

"I'm worried about him," Seth mentioned to Kelly holding her hand. Kelly was a cute, guitar-playing lead singer in a local girl band. She was about 5 feet two inches, thin, very long blonde wavy hair, and had several tattoos on her arms and legs. The tattoos were mostly of butterflies and trees with a unique design surrounding them.

"Well, he seems to be doing okay," Kelly observed.

"Alcohol has that effect on some."

"What are you worried about, Seth?"

Seth took a sip of his beer, "Well, Johnny is known to not take break-ups well. I just don't want him to get back into self-destructive behavior. Hell, he already stopped playing his music, he's drinking excessively. Who knows what he's going to do next?"

"I think you're overreacting a little bit. He seems fine. He's just having a good time. He's found a new place to live, a new roommate, and a friend. This might inspire him to write some new stuff. You must give the man some time. He's been through a lot and it could be a whole lot worse."

"You're right." Seth leaned across the table to kiss Kelly.

Kelly grabbed Seth's chin, "You're so protective of him."

"I love him. He's my friend, my brother. I'd do anything for him."

"I know you would."

Kelly looked over at Lauren who was sitting alone at one of the tables closest to the door. The server brought her another drink and noticed how sad she looked.

"What's wrong, sweetie? You look like you've lost your best friend." It seemed the server noticed as well.

Lauren sighed, "I think I have. My friend over there is not speaking to me," pointing in the direction of Sean. "I didn't tell him that his ex was cheating on him."

"Why didn't you tell him if you were his friend?" The server asked.

"I promised I wouldn't!"

"Promised who?"

"His ex."

"Why?"

"Because I'm his friend too!"

"Well, let me ask you something, are you sure he's *your* friend? Because if you were my friend, I wouldn't put you in a position like that, nor would I withhold that kind of information from someone I considered a friend," the server said. "Something you need to think about."

The server gave her an empathic pat on the shoulder and went to another table leaving Lauren to sit there in her thoughts.

Hours later, Sean and Johnny returned to the apartment. Sean was intoxicated. Johnny only slightly intoxicated, yet it was Sean who was having a difficult time walking and standing up. Hanging on to Johnny, Sean opened the door and they both entered the apartment, where Sean, stumbling over his own feet, almost lost his balance landing face-first on the hardwood floor. Johnny desperately tried to keep Sean upright. He was trying to get him to his bedroom to pass out. On the way to the bedroom, Sean stopped Johnny in the dining room and just stared at him for a moment. Johnny snickered but noticed Sean looking very serious which appeared to come off looking sober, which was not true.

"Sean…"

"Johnny…. I'm a little drunk," Sean slurred.

"Yeah, I've noticed," he grinned.

"Okay, I'm a lot drunk!" Sean exploded with laughter.

Johnny laughed, "I know. Sean, I should…."

Sean closed his eyes and started to fall into Johnny. He stopped him by putting his hands on his chest. Sean opened his eyes slowly and touched one of Johnny's hands looking up into his eyes. Johnny found himself staring back into Sean's bloodshot eyes but was able to see some of his natural eye colors come through. After staring at one another intensely, Sean reached up to Johnny's face and removed his Buddy Holly glasses. Johnny, temporarily distracted by the removing of his glasses, found Sean's hand gently caressing the side of his face. Johnny hesitated for a moment and stepped back.

"Sean, I think I should get you to bed...."

Sean stopped touching Johnny's face. "I don't want to go to bed," Sean was more coherent at this moment.

"I don't think you realize what you're doing." Johnny reasoned.

Sean moved in a little closer to Johnny who was still holding him up, "I know exactly what I'm doing, Johnny."

They were close enough to one another at this point to where their lips were just a whisper away from touching.

"Sean, we shouldn't...I couldn't."

"You're right, we shouldn't, but we then again, maybe you could..."

"I don't think...." Johnny mumbled.

"I think you can," Sean replied boldly.

With some hesitation and heavy breathing between them, Johnny finally gave in and allowed Sean to kiss him. A gentle peck on the lips led to a very passionate, intense kiss, but suddenly Johnny pulled back extending his arms to Sean.

"What? What's wrong?" Sean asked breathing heavily.

"I can't do this. I don't want you to get the wrong idea about me."

"I've thought about nothing but kissing you since that day in the record store...I'm sorry." Sean exhaled.

"Listen, we've both had too much to drink tonight so why don't we just forget about this and go to bed. We can talk about this in the morning with clear heads."

Sean stood there with a sway unable to look at Johnny due to shame of what just happened, "You're right, I'm sorry...so sorry." As he took a deep breath, exhaled collecting himself, he began to walk towards his bedroom when Johnny grabbed his arm turning Sean back to him. They stood there intensely looking at one another. Johnny opened his mouth like he wanted to say something, but nothing came out. Sean anticipated the words that would come out his mouth which took the attention of his eyes. Johnny closed his eyes and leaned his forehead onto Sean's.

"Sean..."

"Johnny..."

Sean noticed Johnny's hands slowly moving toward his waist. Once they contacted his abdomen, Sean got goosebumps all over his body which made him gasp silently. Johnny grabbed the bottom of his shirt, lifted it slowly exposing Sean's lower stomach and chest. Sean was about to say something when Johnny put his hand over his mouth. Sean didn't fight it. He just exhaled and closed his eyes. Johnny removed his hand and slid it behind Sean's head grabbing the back of his hair exposing his neck allowing Johnny to violate it. Sean moaned passionately as he started running his easily Johnny's torso, to his belt, bringing them even closer to one another.

Johnny released Sean's hair and found his way to Sean's lips falling back against the wall. They stopped for a moment catching their breath and looking at each other with such intensity and passion. Even with such directness that got them to this point, Johnny took Sean's hand and led him to his bedroom. Sean felt obliged to follow his lead since he had nowhere else to go nor did he want to be any other place than right there at that very moment.

The Morning After

As the morning light entered Johnny's room, Sean woke up with a pounding headache and a very naked Johnny passed out next to him. In a hangover haze, Sean couldn't help but admire Johnny's back, his tattoos, and shoulder muscles he spent most of the night putting his fingerprints all over and kissing. Sean quietly got out of bed trying not to wake up Johnny and have an uneasy conversation. He grabbed his clothes that were tossed across an armchair. Johnny opened his eyes slowly and noticed he was alone in the bed. As his eyes scanned the room from his sleep position, he noticed Sean tiptoeing across the room towards the door.

From a groggy state, Johnny sat up in the bed noticing Sean, "Hey."

Sean stopped at the foot of the bed, clothes in hand, and nervous, "Hey, how are you? I was trying not to wake you."

Johnny held his head, "Man, I think I'm still drunk. How are you feeling?"

"My head is pounding, but I'm doing okay," Sean scrambled to get himself together. He couldn't help but stare at Johnny's defined chest and stomach. Johnny noticed Sean's eyes fixated on his chest. Johnny looked down, smiled, and rubbed his chest flirtatiously. "See anything you like?"

Sean stammered slightly embarrassed, but after what happened last night, there would be no need now to be shy about admiring Johnny's body. "Nothing! Nothing!"

"It's okay if you look, you know. You did more than just look last night." Johnny joked.

"Yeah, I have a feeling you're right," Sean chuckled.

"It's not a big deal. Listen, Sean, I think we should talk…"

Sean interrupted, "Listen, I'm late for a thing…. I got to go…. hmmm…We will talk later…tonight or even tomorrow…I have to go!" Sean dropped one of his socks, t-shirt, and picked them up while reaching for the door.

"Sean, there's no reason to be so freaked out, but I think we should talk about last night now!"

Sean turned back to Johnny, "We will and I'm not. Just have to go… so we will talk later."

"But…." Johnny mumbled.

Sean opened the door and slammed the door behind him. Johnny fell back onto the bed, put his hands behind his head, and stared at the ceiling fan rotating slowly above him. With a deep sigh, Johnny smiled.

Later that day, Seth met Johnny outside Dirty Inks, a tattoo shop in downtown Burnsville a few blocks from Midnights. They were leaning against the building sitting on their skateboards. He was not sure how well the news would go over with Seth.

"You did what?!?" Seth yelled.

"Will you keep your voice down?" Johnny hushed.

"Johnny, you slept with Sean?"

"Yes! That's what I told you, isn't it?!"

"I don't believe it. So, are you bisexual now?"

Johnny reached for his pack of cigarettes out of his shoulder bag. He offered Seth one, but he denied. "I don't know…. I mean… I don't…I had been drinking. That is why I called you to meet me here. I need to talk to you to help me straighten things out."

Seth scoffed, "Yeah, we need to straighten some things out!"

"Not in the mood right now, Seth."

"Not what I meant. Look, here's the issue. You slept with Sean, but you don't sleep with men. You're all about the ladies. Well, there was that one-time senior year in high school…"

"That's all it was, one time! One time does not a gay make!"

"But it might make a bisexual."

"Meaning?"

"You're very vulnerable right now, with the break-up, the drinking, and this would be the second time that I know of that you've messed around with a man."

Johnny exhaled and put his head in his hands. "I'm going to ask you something and I don't want you to get mad," Seth said cautiously.

Johnny looked at Seth, "Okay?"

"Are you bisexual?"

Johnny turned away from Seth, took a deep inhale from his cigarette, and avoided Seth's question. Seth tugged at Johnny's shirt as he turned back to look at Seth. "Hey, look at me, do you have a feeling for Sean?"

At the apartment, Sean was sitting on the couch in between Mark and Michelle, having the same conversation that Seth and Johnny were having a block away. Sean sat with his head in his hands while Mark and Michelle stared at him.

"You did what?!" Mark yelled.

"With who?!" Michelle yelled back.

"Don't yell at me! My head is pounding like crazy!"

"I bet your ass is too especially after…" Michelle quipped.

Mark reached pass Sean and poked Michelle in the arm, "Not helping here."

Michelle cleared her throat, "I'm sorry. Sean, you need to talk to Johnny."

"What the hell happened?" Mark asked.

Sean sighed, "We were drunk. Well, I was drunk, but we both were drinking…and it just happened. We were talking, then talking lead to some touching, touching lead to some kissing and…. well you can probably figure the rest out from there."

"Sean, you can't be sleeping with your straight roommate. You need to work this out and make sure you haven't ruined a friendship or worst lose a roommate over this." Mark said.

Michelle patted Sean on his shoulders, bringing him close to her. "Okay, this doesn't seem important. You both were drinking and did something stupid. It's over and it's not going to happen again, right? So, I say forget about it!"

"Of course, it's a big deal, and neither one of us can just forget about it! It got way too deep to just forget about it without talking about it."

"You know, maybe this is his way of trying something new? I mean, he did get his heartbroken by a girl, maybe being with a guy was something he had always thought about, wanted to try, and you were the lucky recipient?" Mark said.

"If you want to try something new, you get a new haircut, buy some new clothes or in his case, get another tattoo. You don't go and sleep with your gay roommate!" Michelle said.

"Maybe sleeping with Sean was something not so new to him."

Sean frustrated, "My head hurts. I can't deal with this right now."

Michelle ran her fingers through Sean's hair, "Sweetie, I'm going to ask you something and don't want you to get mad, but do you like Johnny?"

Sean thought for a moment, "No…. I don't…maybe…not really."

"Look, just talk to him. Get things out in the open."

"I will." Sean paused, "This morning he wanted to talk about last night, but I kept interrupting him because I'm not sure if I wanted to hear what he had to say."

"Why?" Mark asked.

"I don't know. I just wanted to get out of there."

"Well, there was your opportunity to talk to him about what happened. He seemed willing to talk about it. Now, you just need to get your head out of your arse and talk to him!"

Sean sighed, "Yeah, I know. I just couldn't take my eyes off him lying in that bed looking at me all normal, no weird expressions or reactions. He just looked at me as if everything was okay, everything was great!"

Michelle interrupted, "I bet he looked amazing naked."

Sean and Mark turned to Michelle in disgust. Michelle noticed the look on their faces, "What? Like I'm the only one thinking it."

Sean smiled, "He was just so nice and very comforting. I almost forgot what it felt like." Sean got up from the couch and walked over to the dining room table. "He's just so masculine, handsome, kind and sweet and……. I shouldn't have feelings or thoughts about Johnny!"

"Feelings?" Mark questioned.

"Thoughts?" Michelle questioned as well.

Sean sighed, "I'm in trouble, aren't I?"

A week had passed and there was no sign of Johnny. Sean knocked on his bedroom door hoping he decided to come home to at least to sleep. Sean didn't get an answer, so he opened the door slowly and investigated the room. He walked into the room with caution and started looking around. Any evidence he could find that Johnny was there would at least let him know that he was okay. Sean walked over to the bed and examined it as if it were a crime scene. He turned, extended his arms outwards, and fell back onto it. The moment he fell, he immediately smelled Johnny. He was all over the bed and now all over him. He embraced that moment along with last night by wrapping himself in the comforter and top sheet. He reached for the pillow at the head of the bed, put it to his face and inhaled. He held the pillow close to his chest as if it were Johnny. He held it looking at the ceiling fan rotating above him. He closed his eyes and reminisced about the night before.

After a few minutes, Sean opened his eyes, put back the pillow, and got up off the bed. He left the room and walked out to the kitchen to fix him something to eat. Just before he could make it to the kitchen, the phone rang in the living room. Sean ran to pick it up before the machine got it.

"Hello?"

"Hey Sean, it's Seth."

Sean sat in the comforter covered recliner, "Hey. What's up?"

"I was wondering if you wouldn't mind meeting me at Midnights for a beer. I would like to talk to you."

"Um, sure. What time?"

"Twenty minutes?"

"I'll see you then."

Sean hung up the phone. He got up from the recliner to head to the kitchen when there was a knock at the door. He did a quick turn to get the door. When he opened it, it was the last person he expected to see that day or ever in that case. Lauren stood there, no makeup, eyes red and puffy, hair not combed and wearing cutoff shorts and a sweatshirt two sizes too big.

"I know you're probably still mad…"

"You're right," Sean responded stone-faced to Lauren's correct assumption.

"I would understand if you slammed the door in my face right…"

Without hesitation, that's exactly what Sean did. He began to walk back to the kitchen, then stopped, exhaled, turned back, and opened the door to see Lauren on her knees crying. "What do you want, Lauren?" Sean said coldly.

"I'm so sorry that I didn't tell you about Jaime, okay?! When he told me what was going on, I swore that I wouldn't tell you. He knew we were all friends and he said if we wanted to stay that way that it would best if I kept my mouth shut which is that's what I did. I am not proud of what I did. I sat back and watched him hurt you and lie to you. I did the same thing; when you poured your heart out to me that night at Midnights, I sat back and said nothing when I had many opportunities to do so! I will never forgive myself for that. I'm truly sorry and I do wish I could make it better." Lauren cried.

Sean, emotionless, took a moment and with a sigh responded, "I appreciate what you came here to say, but you know what you can do to make it better. You could leave!"

"Sean, we've been friends for far too long to throw that away."

"Correction, we *were* friends. No more!"

"May I come in for a minute?"

"Oh, hell no!"

"Please?"

"Look, I have other things to worry about than whether I'm going to keep a friendship with a two-faced bitch like you!"

"I know I did you wrong, but that's no reason to say such hurtful things to me. I have feelings too, you know."

"Did you ever consider my feelings, Lauren?! Fuck your feelings!" Sean slammed the door in Lauren's face.

Ally was walking home through the park and noticed a guy sitting on the bench playing guitar. This guy had on a hooded sweatshirt, camouflage pants, and Chuck Taylors. She was going to keep walking but realized that she recognized this guy; especially the music he was playing.

"I didn't realize you had reached celebrity status since apparently everyone is looking for you." She said to the hooded guy.

The guy stopped playing the guitar, looked up at Ally, and pulled the hood off his head, "And yet you found me!"

"Johnny! Where have you been?! You haven't been to work in days! Everyone is worried sick about you!"

"I slept with Sean."

"Whoa, no shit?"

"No shit..."

Ally sighed and sat next to Johnny. Johnny sat his guitar on the opposite side of himself.

"Johnny..."

"I'm not gay, Ally."

"I wasn't going to ask you that, but you did sleep with Sean."

They sat there in silence next to one another, avoiding eye contact as much as possible.

Johnny finally looked at Ally, "I do like him. I guess I let what happened that night happen because deep down inside I wanted it. I've been telling myself that for days. Funny, it's the first time I've ever said that out loud."

Ally leaned and kissed Johnny on the cheek. "I'm happy that you found someone, be it, friend or lover, however, you categorize it. The point is that you're playing music again."

"All I've been doing is playing chords on this guitar, thinking of a song while thinking of him. You're not going to judge me, tell me what a mistake I'm making and that I'm not thinking straight....no pun intended."

Ally winked at Johnny, "Not my style. I'm your friend and I'm going to be here for you no matter what. If you're happy and you like Sean as more than a friend, then that's great! I'm happy for you."

"You don't think I'll be making his life more complicated, do you?"

"Have you thought about how all this is going to complicate *your* life? I mean, you just got your heart crushed not too long ago. Plus, now you're saying that you're bisexual. You have feelings for this guy!"

"I guess I am."

"So, Sean is what you want?"

"Yeah, I think so."

Ally stared at Johnny as he picked up his guitar and started playing again with a huge smile on his face. "From the sound of it, yes, I think you know what you want." She hugged Johnny as he continued to play.

At Midnights, Sean was sitting at a bar table waiting for Seth. Twenty minutes later, Seth finally arrived.

"Hey, thanks for meeting me."

"Sure, even though I'm not sure why we're meeting in the first place."

"Well, I thought we could talk. Maybe if we put our heads together, we could figure out where Johnny is. Have you heard from him?"

"No. I was hoping you would've heard something. I've been waiting by the phone just in case he called. Isn't that funny?"

"Hilarious," Seth said sarcastically.

"What's your problem?"

The server brought over some waters, "You guys ready to order?"

"I'll just have a beer, please," Sean said.

"Same for me."

The server walked over to the bar where he gave the order to the bartender. Sean noticed Seth staring at him unpleasantly "Is there a problem?"

Seth scoffed, "Where do you get off making a move on someone you know is straight?"

"Ah, I take it you know about the other night." Sean sighed.

"Yeah, I know! It's a pretty shitty thing to do to someone who was just trying to be a good roommate and friend to you; taking advantage of someone who isn't into dudes..."

"Seth...."

"I mean, what did you expect to accomplish that night?" Seth interrupted. "Were you just horny and wanted to closest available piece of man-ass you could get your hands on; which just happened to be your straight roommate?!"

"Wait a minute...."

"Now, with all that said, I know what happened that night was *not* entirely all your fault. I've known Johnny for a long time now, and I know he wouldn't do anything that he truly felt in his heart he didn't want to do." Seth hesitated for a moment, "Let's just say this is not the first time something like this happened."

"Wait! Johnny's been with a guy before?"

"It was in high school. They just kissed, but it never went this far. Johnny's running off and not telling anyone where he is; I don't know what that's about. Listen, I'm sorry for being harsh there for a moment, but there's something more going on here between you two than just friends and just roommates."

"Do you think that I'm the only one thinking everything is okay here? I'm worried too, not to mention just as confused as he must be. I've never slept with a straight guy before; let alone a roommate. This isn't easy for me or anyone involved! Within two months, I've gotten dumped, lost my best friend, slept with my roommate! Trust me; this is not a picnic in the park for me!"

"Sean, I realize that what you've been through was tough, but you have to realize what Johnny has gone through was tough as well."

"I know that! That is why we connected so well. We were able to talk and relate to one another."

"The girl that he loved for three years cheated on him. This was the girl that he was going to marry. Then suddenly, it's all over just like that! He told me about what happened to you and you're right, you guys have something in common. You both were able to be there for one another and help each other. I believe that."

The server came by the table with their beers. They each took a sip of them.

"I like him, Seth," Sean confessed.

Seth looked up from his glass and set it down, "Well, I don't think you'd be alone in this one."

"What should I do?" Sean sighed and sat his beer down.

"How the hell do I know? You two need to talk this out!"

"That would be great if I knew where he was."

"When he's ready, he'll come back. Just needs some time."

"So, what do I do in the meantime?"

"Drink your beer and shut up!"

Sean smiled and took another sip of beer and glanced out the window observing the people traffic; hoping that just maybe Johnny would walk by.

Sean left Midnights feeling a little better; especially after talking to Seth, whom he left at the bar to talk to a few bandmates that showed up an hour prior. As he was walking back to the apartment, he saw the back of a guy wearing a black sweater and pants standing there outside of a bar on the phone. As he got closer, he realized the guy was Jaime. Jaime turned around noticing Sean walking towards him.

"You've got to be kidding me…" Sean said disgustedly.

Jaime grinned, "Ha! What is this? Are you stalking me now?"

Sean walked around Jaime as he proceeded to follow, "Don't flatter yourself."

"Coming from a hot date?"

"That's none of your business," Sean answered sharply.

Jaime caught up with Sean and stepped in front of him. "What's your hurry, sweetie?"

"I'm allergic to bull shit. Now if you'll excuse me…" Sean moved around trying his best to avoid confrontation with him. Jaime turned quick and got in front of Sean yet again, "Come on now, Sean…."

This time Sean didn't move, he got right up in Jaime's face, "Get the hell away from me…NOW!"

"It sounds like that roommate of yours is having some effect on you. If I wasn't scared of him, what makes you think I'd fear you?"

Sean grabbed Jaime by the throat and threw him against the side of the building. Sean squeezed as Jaime gasped with fright which made him squeezed even harder. "You should be scared. How does it feel? How does it feel not having control over me anymore?"

"Sean…please…. I'll scream."

Sean became more enraged and squeezed harder as Jaime whimpered, "I dare you…"

Jaime shuttered and started to cry. Sean leaned into Jaime almost touching nose to nose. "Now who's pathetic?"

Sean was still holding Jaime's throat against the wall when a beautiful girl with short brown hair, blue eyes ran up between them. Sean looked at the girl and back at Jaime, but then Sean looked at the girl again with familiarity. Sean released him. Jaime gasped and fell to the ground coughing as the girl ran to his side.

"Who are you? What are you doing to my boyfriend? I'm calling the cops," she said to Sean.

She pulled her cell phone out of her purse. Sean had been shocked and surprised, but not like this, "It was you." Sean said pointing to Jaime.

Jaime managed to get out a word still trying to catch his breath, "What?"

She stopped dialing the police and put down her cell phone as if something instinctual told her to do so, "What's going on? Who's this guy?" She asked Jaime.

Sean looked at Jaime, who now stopped coughing. Sean laughed as he walked towards the entrance of his building, "Jaime. You should think about changing your cologne. It tends to linger when you're fucking someone else's girlfriend in their shower! Nice to meet you…Natalie, I presumed? I'll tell Johnny you said hello."

Jaime's face lost all color and suddenly couldn't breathe again. He fell into Natalie's arms, "Jaime, what's going on? How does he know my name and how does he know about Johnny? Jaime?"

Sean remembered seeing a picture of Johnny and Natalie the first day he moved into the apartment in one of his boxes. After tonight, he put it all together and realized that he and Johnny's exes were cheating with one another. For some reason, that gave Sean a little bit of amusement.

Sean entered his building. As Sean started going up the stairs, he saw Lauren sitting at the top of the stairs. He stopped as they looked at one another. He exhaled and continued to go up the stairs. Lauren stood up, "Before you say anything, please just let me tell you how sorry I am."

"Okay."

"Okay?" Lauren surprised.

"Yes. I forgive you." Sean started to walk around her to get to his apartment.

"Wait! You're not mad at me anymore?"

Sean turned to Lauren, "Nope."

"Does that mean we're friends again?"

"I wouldn't go that far, but we'll see."

"I promise! Never!" Lauren, still surprised and shocked, didn't want to question Sean's decision anymore.

"Good. I'm tired. I'm going to go to bed. We will talk later."

"Really?" Lauren smiled.

"Good night," Sean got his keys out of pocket, opened the door, and closed it behind him. Lauren went down the stairs leaving the building.

Sean stood in the foyer and noticed something different in the dark apartment with the light coming through the windows. He slowly walked into the living room looking around noticing the recliner was gone, replaced with a new black suede armchair. He threw his keys on the coffee table, walked around the chair running his fingers along the top, and sat down gently into it. He leaned back, exhaled, and closed his eyes. Suddenly, from down the hall, he heard a guitar playing. He looked down the hallway and saw light coming from Johnny's room. He leaned back, closed his eyes again, and smiled. The music got closer and louder. It stopped and just then Sean felt two hands come down on his shoulder making their way down to his chest. Sean didn't move but got a chill from a whisper in his ear, "Welcome home."

Sean reached his arms above him and around Johnny's neck, turned, and kissed him on the cheek. Johnny came around the chair, sat on top of him and they began to kiss passionately. Sean caressed the back of Johnny's head, "I should be saying that to you!" They continued kissing as the moonlight entered the apartment accenting their artwork on the wall. The leaves brushed against the windowsills as the wind picked them off the trees. Fall had made itself at home in Burnsville. With the changing of the leaves brought new and exciting changes in the lives of her residents. Seasons change…and people do as well.

Part Two

New Life

It was a lovely warm spring night. The trees were plump full of life as the mountains of Burnsville were covered with a blanket of brilliant greens. Flowers bloomed allowing their perfume to waft through the air like the freshly baked apple pie sitting on the window ledge of a Norman Rockwell painting. The winter jackets came off and sleeveless shirts and sandals came out of the closet once again. Picnics in the park during the day and drum circles in the evening brought the best of young and old. It was night walking downtown or in West Burnsville with ice cream instead of hot chocolate. Two years had passed as another winter had made its season finale and welcomed a new season to Burnsville… Spring.

Ally and Seamus were sitting at an outside table eating dinner at Diego's, a hip and upcoming restaurant in downtown Burnsville. Since they had just finished a delicious Osso Bucco with fresh, steamed vegetables and roasted garlic Romano cheese risotto, Seamus decided he wanted to have her for dessert. He began kissing all over her neck and shoulders. They had been secretly dating for a year now. As much as Seamus was enjoying Ally, she was not complaining in the least, "Easy tiger. Control yourself. Someone might see us," she giggled.

"Who Ally? Who's going to walk by and see this very attractive couple making out?"

Seamus' very handsome yet rough-tough exterior could be seen playing rugby in the park on Saturdays or skateboarding with Johnny around West Burnsville with no shirt on in the summer months. This was usually a welcoming sight for pedestrians and shop owners alike. He had a smile that had women fall in love instantly, but his heart only belonged to one woman faithfully; Ally.

Ally pushed Seamus back and looked around suspiciously, "Hey, we need to be a little bit more discreet in public. No one knows about us."

"And why is that, Ally? I'm getting sick and tired having to hide how I feel about you in public. We both like one another so what's wrong with telling everyone that?" Seamus expressed aggravated.

"Nothing, I just don't want to make a big production out of it!"

"Are you seeing someone else?" Seamus suspected.

"No, I'm just seeing you!"

"Then there's no need for this conversation." Seamus moved in on Ally and kissed her forcefully, yet sexually. Things became to get hot and a little inappropriate for public viewing. The other patrons and people that passed by began to stare at the couple giggling and mumbling something under their breath. Ally looked around and became nervous. She whispered, "Hey, let's go back to my place."

"Okay." Seamus pulled out his wallet to pay the check. "By the way, what time do you want me to pick you up for Michelle's art show?"

"Did we make plans to go together? I was going to go with Johnny and Sean." Ally said adjusting her dress straps.

"Well, you can go with me; now that we're a couple."

"Why don't I just meet you there? Cool?"

Seamus threw some money down and abruptly got up from the table, "Have a good night."

"Hey, where are you going?" She called out to him. She got up from the table and followed behind him up the street.

"I'm not playing games with you anymore! Until you feel comfortable telling others about us, we're over!"

"Seamus!" Ally caught up with him and stopped him, "Look, I'm sorry, but I'm not playing games with you. I'm just afraid of committing myself to someone and getting hurt."

"How can you be so sure I'm going to hurt you, Ally?"

"I'm not sure of that! And I'm not saying you will. I'm just scared. Seamus, please be patient with me. I'm open to the idea of us every day. I even told my boss the other day about you. That counts for something, right?"

Seamus scoffed, "That's nice, but not enough. I want you to be comfortable enough to tell your friends and family about us…especially me.

"My friends know you."

"Your friends know me as the bartender at Midnights. They don't know me as the man that has spent every night for a year in your bed!"

Ally began acting coy while playing with Seamus' shirt, "Why are you making such a thing about this?"

Seamus ignored her coyness, "If you can't see why then there's a problem."

"Alright, I'll tell Johnny. Are you happy now?" Ally sighed.

"Don't patronize me! It doesn't matter who you tell if in your eyes you don't see me as part of your life! Ally, can't you see that I've fallen for you?"

Ally stunned, "You've fallen for me?"

Seamus put his arms around her, "Of course! You're all I want. I want to be the man that makes you happy and I want everyone we know and those around us to know that, but most importantly, you need to know and realize that. Ally, don't you think a year is long enough to remain silent and keep me at a distance? I've been patient long enough, don't you think?"

Ally smiled and touched the side of Seamus' face, "I do think it has been long enough." Ally looked deep into his eyes and finally saw what she should have seen a long time ago, a good man that wanted nothing but happiness and love for her. "Okay, let's tell our friends. Fuck let's tell everyone!

Seamus kissed her, "Are we officially a couple now?

"If you want to label this then, yes, we're a couple." Ally giggled.

"No more secret sex?"

"I thought that was the best part of this relationship?" Ally joked.

Seamus motioned to his crotch, "I believe you've been acquainted with the best part of this relationship."

Ally moved her hands easily to his crotch, "It looks as if someone wants to come out and play!" She said teasing him.

"Oh, we're always up for playing with you!"

"There's something to be said about good playmates," she moaned continuing to fondle him.

Seamus started to breathe heavily and moan, "Instead of going back to your place, let's go to Midnights! It doesn't open for hours. We can violate the manager's office again!"

"Tempting, but let's violate the bar!" Ally grabbed his hand and they both ran off in the direction of the bar.

"The bar! Where on the stage?"

"I was thinking more on top of the bar. There are some places where you haven't had whiskey yet."

Seamus stopped and let go of Ally's hand. He started to think and realize this situation could have great possibilities. He exhaled and bit down on his fist, "Damn, I love you." She came back to grab him, and both ran off to Midnights.

Later that night in a dream, Sean stood in front of the bathroom sink looking into the mirror. He was wearing nothing but boxers. His left and right arms extended out in the front of him and his wrists were cut. He was bleeding into the sink and the bathroom counter. The cordless phone lay on the bathroom counter covered in blood. It rang twice slightly muffled but getting louder as the ringing continued. Sean looked at himself in the mirror with tears running down his face. The phone stopped ringing and then began to ring twice. He answered the phone but remained silent. A hand came up behind him and rested on Sean's shoulder. A male voice over the phone finally said, "Forgive me."

Sean sat up in bed, sweating profusely and gasping for air. He grabbed his chest and exhaled. He frantically looked at his wrist and noticed they were uncut. He wiped his forehead and looked over to the other side of the bed to see Johnny sleeping. He had been having these bad dreams for about a year. After settling back down, he snuggled up against Johnny wrapping his arms around his stomach, "Another bad dream?" Johnny asked half awake.

"Yeah," Sean exhaled.

"The same one?"

"Yeah."

Johnny yawned, "I'm worried about you. You've been having this dream for some time now."

Sean was having a difficult time telling Johnny about the real dream he had been having. He told Johnny when he started having this dream that it was about Johnny being involved in a terrible car accident and him dying in his arms.

Sean and Johnny had been living together now for two years. They moved out of Sean's downtown apartment and into an apartment in West Burnsville. Ally had recommended the twelve-story apartment building in the heart of the art district of West Burnsville for two reasons; first, Sean had always wanted to live in West Burnsville and because now they all will be neighbors. Ally lives one floor below them.

Sean took a deep breath, "I'm good. I think I should see that psychologist Michelle told me about."

"Do you want me to come with you?"

"No, I'll be okay. Go back to sleep, baby."

The next day, Sean, wearing one of Johnny's vintage tee and knee-long cargo shorts, was walking downtown with Ally. They were going to Daddy Pimp's to check out some vinyl. As they started to look through records, Ally noticed several records that interested her; Led Zeppelin, The Doors, and David Bowie. Ally felt today would be a good time to tell Sean that she was seeing Seamus, but she hadn't quite worked up the nerve to say it out loud. She knew Sean would be happy and supportive of her, she just didn't know how to say it. Plus, she knew he had something on his mind that he might want to talk about allowing Ally more time to procrastinate. Sean hadn't found anything that interested him. He was just flipping through the albums trying to get that dream out of his head. Ally and Sean found themselves aisles across from one another.

"So, are you still having that dream?" Ally mentioned flipping through records.

"Yes."

"When do you see that psychologist?"

"I made an appointment for next week. I just don't understand why I keep having this dream. It's bothering me."

"Well, hopefully, this psychologist will be able to help you."

Sean flipped through a stack of records and finally saw something that appealed to him. "Yeah, I guess you're right."

"How long have you been having this dream now?"

"A year. I think everyone is getting sick of hearing about it."

"Everyone?" Ally asked skeptically.

Sean looked at Ally who was still flipping through records, "What's that supposed to mean?"

"Have you told Johnny what you have been dreaming about?"

Sean went back to looking through the records trying to ignore Ally's question. Ally stopped looking at records, walked over to Sean's aisle staring him down, "Well?"

"Well, what? No…."

"Why not? You've told everyone that you know and even some of Johnny's friends, but you haven't told your boyfriend whom you've been living with for two years?"

"No! I haven't!"

"Yeah, you need to see that psychologist because there's something not right in your head."

Ally got her records and walked up to the cashier. Sean, with only one record, followed. "There's nothing wrong with me. I just don't want him to see my dream as a sign of weakness."

"What? That's the dumbest thing I've ever heard. Johnny has seen you and been there for you at your lowest. Do we need to revisit the great breakup of 2008? The man is very understanding and has always been supportive of you, not to mention he's very easy to talk to. The operative word there is 'talk'."

"Now you're a psychologist?"

"It's common sense! Talk to the man…. that's why he's there."

Ally got her receipt and records and stood next to Sean as he paid for his stuff. He tried to find the most sensible reason he couldn't tell Johnny, "It's just something I can't express to him. I don't know why," he exhaled.

"Well, a secret is a good way to end a relationship." Ally realized what she was saying and thought she didn't have room to tell Sean about secrets since she was keeping one herself.

"It's not a secret!"

Ally stopped Sean, "Does he know about the real dream that everyone else around him already knows?"

Sean stood there stumped at Ally's question, "No."

"Then it's a secret! You're keeping information from him and you made up some dream, so you didn't have to tell him the real one you've been having! That's a lie! You need to sit Johnny down and tell him….and you need to do this before you go see the psychologist!"

Sean sighed in frustration as they left the record store. Ally and Sean started to window shop as they walked down the street.

Sean sighed, "Alright, I'll tell him. I don't think he's going to like what I have to say."

"Well, you might have to deal with the fact that he'll be angry with you for lying to him about this, but Johnny is forgiving, he will listen, he will understand, and he will still be there when it's all over. "She put her arm around Sean as they walked down the street to her car.

"I know he will. Thanks." Sean smiled.

"So, what are your plans for the rest of the day?"

"I'm meeting Craig at the Student Union. We're studying for an exam we have next week."

"Ah, Craig. Has he come out of the closet yet?" Ally joked.

"For the last time, the man is *not* gay!"

Ally stopped Sean and held the sides of his face, "Sean, the man is gay and has a crush on you…. period. And yes, it's that obvious!"

Sean took Ally's hands off his face and continued to walk, "Ally, just because everyone wants him to be gay doesn't mean he is!"

"Ah, this would include you! I do recall you wishing he was gay when you first met him."

"You were so drunk; I'm surprised you even remembered that conversation. That was four years ago. He's my best friend now. We're like brothers…and I'm telling you, the man is straight! He's with girls all the time!

"Really? You're going to use that as a logical reason. I do believe you're now dating someone that used to be with girls all the time as well."

Sean cleared his throat, "I see your point, but I sincerely don't think the man has a crush on me. That's just ridiculous."

"Just calling them as I see them."

"Well, I just don't see it."

"Why, because he doesn't like Madonna or Cher?"

"I've just never gotten that vibe from him."

"Again, need I remind you…."

Sean interrupted, "Alright, alright! I get your point!"

They walked up to Ally's car as she looked for her keys in her purse, "If he was gay, I wouldn't be surprised because he's so fucking hot!"

Sean laughed, "I know it would be another score for our team."

"First Johnny…now maybe Craig. It's just not fair," sighed Ally.

Sean shrugged, "Since when has sexuality been fair?"

"Amen to that. Okay, I'm out of here. Happy studying and call me later!"

Ally got in her car and Sean stepped back as she started up the car. Ally rolled down the window, "Hey, tell Johnny about the dream….and while you're at it, find out what the deal is with Craig."

Sean laughed, "Sure!"

Ally drove off as Sean walked to campus.

Auditions

Later that afternoon, Seth, Johnny, and some other band members were holding auditions at Midnights for a new male singer for the band. Johnny and Seth were sitting at the bar across from the stage. There was a long table in front of the stage where the other band members were judging the auditions. The singers were patiently waiting at the cocktail tables that surrounded the stage and along the bar. Johnny looked distracted all afternoon which was clear to Seth, "Alright, what's the deal with you today?"

"Have you noticed anything strange about Sean lately?" Johnny asked.

Seth scoffed, "Why are you asking me? You live with him."

"I mean, has he said anything out of the ordinary to you lately?"

"Um, no…. Why?"

Johnny shook it off, "Nothing. Never mind."

Seth looked at his watch impatiently, "Are we almost done here?"

"We have four more singers to audition. Relax."

"We've been at this for two hours now. I'm hungry and getting crankier by the minute….and I want a beer!"

We'll get something to eat and some beers after the auditions, but we need to find a lead singer, so chill out!" Johnny laughed.

"I'm chill. I'm just hungry. Will you please tell me what was wrong with you as our lead singer?"

"I want to play more. The lead singer thing was only temporary. It was never supposed to go on this long."

"Yeah, but we've done great with you at lead vocals. People love your voice and the gigs have been sold out because of it!"

"I would also like to think that my music had something to do with that, not just my voice. Don't worry, we'll find someone for lead vocals."

Seth sighed, "I just don't know why we can't hire Kelly to be lead vocals. It would save us a whole lot of time."

"Well, for one, Kelly has her band and it's really hard to be our lead vocalist when you're in California. Not to mention, why would you want your ex-girlfriend singing in our band?"

"There are no hard feelings between us. She decided to move out to California, and I decided to stay here. We both agreed that long-distance relationships don't work, so we ended it. No big deal. It was a nice thought though."

"It was a crazy thought, but even with the breakup, I do see the flame still burns bright for a certain guitar-playing blond!" Johnny teased.

Seth cleared his throat, "I don't think so. I hardly think about her anymore."

"Yeah right," Johnny smirked.

"Oh, shut up and pick a singer already, will you?"

When the singer finished, the other band members called out for the next audition. A tall, skinny guy with tattoos and hair covering his eyes stepped on the stage. As he started to sing, it amazed everyone how his stage presence and voice was reminiscent of Johnny's. He wore a t-shirt with Metallica logo and baggy cargo shorts, something he might've gotten out of Johnny's closet. Johnny and Seth's attention were no longer on Kelly and Sean, but this singer.

Johnny nudged Seth in the arm, "Now I think we are getting somewhere".

"Damn, he's good!"

"I think we might have found our new lead singer."

"I second that."

Seth stopped the audition. They walked up to the stage to meet their new lead singer. "Hey man, great stuff. What's your name?" Seth asked.

"Tagger!"

Seth and Johnny introduced themselves to Tagger, "Nice to meet you. I'm Seth and this is Johnny."

Tagger got excited when he was introduced to Johnny, "Yeah, yes, I know who *you* are! I mean, I've followed you guys for years now. You're amazing. Your voice is what made me want to become a singer in the first place. I'm a big fan. When I saw you were holding auditions for a new lead singer, I couldn't resist!"

Seth noticed something going on. He noticed that Tagger was still shaking Johnny's hand while gushing over him just a little too much. Johnny finally noticed it as well and released his hand.

"Oh, I'm sorry. I'm just so excited to meet you. I just love you guys," Tagger said addressing the band. He turned back to Johnny still nervous, "I love your songs and your style!"

Tagger caught himself staring into Johnny's deep green eyes which made Johnny somewhat uncomfortable, but Johnny couldn't resist looking back into his bluish-gray eyes disguised my strands of long blond hair and long eyelashes, "Thanks, man. I appreciate that."

"Ahem! Tagger! Could you please excuse us for one moment?" Seth asked.

"Um…sure."

Seth pulled Johnny away by his arm towards the bar. The other band members jumped on the stage to introduce themselves to Tagger.

"What the hell is going on?"

"What?" Johnny wondered.

"The man is flirting with you."

"No, he's not."

"It's completely obvious and if I wasn't mistaken, you were flirting back!"

Johnny stunned, "I *was* not!"

"If I wouldn't have intervened just then, you guys would have been doing it on the stage!"

"You're crazy! Have you forgotten that I'm with Sean?"

"Have you? I'm telling you that man up there has the hots for you!"

Johnny changed the subject, "Are we hiring him or not?"

"That's up to you! You're the boss!"

"Okay, I guess we found our new lead singer."

"Yay! Now, can we please go get something to eat and get drunk?"

They went back to the stage to join the other band members. Tagger stepped off to the side where he was talking on the phone. Tagger noticed Seth and Johnny had returned and hung up the phone walking back over to join the guy, "I'm sorry, my girlfriend was wondering how the auditions were going."

"Well, you can call her back and let her know that you're our new lead singer," Seth said.

Tagger excited, "Really? Holy shit! Yes!

The band members clapped in congratulations as Tagger jumped up and down with excitement.

Johnny shook Tagger's hand, "Congratulations."

"Thank you. Thanks, guys! This is great!"

"Well, just don't stand there, call your girlfriend and give her the good news!" Seth cheered. "Alright, now that we got a new lead singer, let's go eat and get drunk!"

They all shouted in agreement, gathered up their belongings, and began to leave. Tagger stood in the corner on the phone while Johnny started cleaning up the papers and empty glasses. Tagger got off the phone to help Johnny.

"Oh, you don't have to do that," Johnny said.

"Hey, I'm part of the band now. Let me help you."

Johnny laughed, "Yes, you are part of the band, so you are obligated to go get something to eat and get drunk with the rest of the band."

"Sounds good, but I'll wait for you if that is okay?"

"Oh, I'm not going. I have other plans, so you better go and catch up with them."

Tagger seemed a little disappointed by this news, "Oh, okay."

Johnny looked at his watch and realized what time it was, "Speaking of, I'm late!"

"Date?" Tagger asked.

Johnny laughed, "No, well, sort of. I'm meeting my boyfriend for dinner."

"Boyfriend?"

"Yeah," Johnny smiled.

Tagger stopped cleaning and stood there staring at the floor. Johnny noticed him looking disappointed, "You alright?"

"Yeah, I just didn't know that...."

"Know what? That I had a boyfriend or that I was bisexual?"

Tagger cleared his throat, "Both, I guess."

"Well, I am. It's no big deal."

"How long have you two been together?"

"Two years."

"Oh, wow, that's great."

Johnny quickly changed the subject as he put the glasses on the bar, "So, how about you? How long have you and your girlfriend been together?"

"We just started dating several months ago."

"Does it look promising?"

"Too soon to tell, but we'll see!"

"Right on, man. Come on, let's get out of here."

Johnny turned off the lights and grabbed his skateboard and guitar. Tagger grabbed his bag and skateboard as they left the bar. As they walked down the street with their skateboards under their arms, they were having a conversation about skating and music. There were plenty of laughs between them and even moments of showing one another their scars from performing skateboarding stunts gone badly. Johnny put his guitar over his shoulder as Tagger got quiet looking at the different stores they passed, "Johnny, can I ask you something?

"Sure."

"How did you and your boyfriend meet, if I'm not being too personal?"

Johnny smiled, "Not at all. We were roommates and one night after drinking, we fooled around, then two years later, here we are!"

"Oh wow. We're you always attracted to him?"

"At first, no. I had just gotten out of a three-year relationship with a girl I wanted to marry. I moved out of our apartment and moved in with Sean since he was looking for a roommate. He had just gotten out a relationship as well. We became friends. I don't know, out of friendship grew attraction, I guess…and inspiration…and I've never been happier!"

Johnny began to laugh which boosted Tagger's curiosity, "What's so funny?"

"Nothing," Johnny laughed.

"So, this girl, your ex, pushed you into the arms of a man."

Johnny laughed even harder, "You can say that! I guess I've always had these feelings deep down inside. It just took that cheating bitch and a good man like Sean to bring them to surface."

"Sean? So, the mystery man has a name."

Johnny grinned, "He's no mystery, more like someone special."

"Well, Sean looks like he makes you happy. Just the mention of his name or to even talk about him just lights you up."

"You know what Tag, I'm very happy…. for the first time in a long time, very happy."

"Tag? No one has called me that in forever! I like it. I think it's cool that you found someone that makes you truly happy." Tagger smiled.

"How about you? Does your girlfriend make you happy?"

"Granted we've only been dating for several months, but yes, I'm happy."

Johnny was confused because he noticed Tagger forcing a smile as well as a response. He felt that he might not be telling him the complete truth about his relationship, but since they just met, Johnny just let it go and smiled. They approached The Grill, a neighborhood restaurant and bar where they were meeting the rest of the band members. Seth saw them outside and ran to greet them, "Come on you guys! Beer's getting warm," Seth announced followed up by a loud belch.

Johnny laughed and shook his head, "Tagger, from the sounds of it, you've got some catching up to do."

"Hello, have we met?" Seth asked Johnny sarcastically, "Now come on, you guys have pitchers waiting!"

"Pitchers? Have we been gone that long?" Tagger joked.

"Oh, I should've warned you that Seth and the band can put down some beer!"

"Shit, what have I gotten myself into?" Tagger asked Johnny jokingly.

Seth threw his arm around Tagger and Johnny, "Good times that's what! Now come on, both of you!"

Johnny patted Tagger on the back, "Tagger is going to join you guys. I'm meeting Sean for dinner."

"Well, I guess I'll see you guys later for movie night?" Seth asked leaning on to Tagger.

"Yeah, just remember it's your turn to bring the movies. Also, try not to get too drunk. Save some room for tonight, please?"

"I won't, and I will…. don't worry."

"Alright." Johnny gave Tagger a firm handshake, "It was nice meeting you. Welcome to the band!"

"Thanks…and thank you for the conversation. I look forward to more great talks and laughs."

Johnny started to walk away when he quickly turned back around, "Don't forget creating great music together. See you guys later!" Johnny got on his skateboard and skated off. Tagger stood there as Johnny skated away. Tagger and Seth went inside the restaurant. Before they reached the table where the other members were sitting, Tagger stopped Seth, "Hey, what movies are you guys watching tonight?"

That afternoon on campus, Sean and Craig were sitting in the Student Union studying for their exam. As they were studying, Sean noticed Craig daydreaming about something other than World Literature. Sean waved his hand in front of his face, "Hey, you're supposed to be studying! What are you thinking about over there?"

"Oh, right, sorry. "Craig's attention went back into his textbook.

"So, what were you thinking about?" Sean asked.

"Nothing," Craig said.

"Bullshit. Try again."

Craig smiled, "I was just thinking about how we're about to graduate in a few months. I can still remember our freshman year as if it were yesterday."

"Believe me I'm trying to forget!" Sean smiled, "I know we need to pass this exam next week or we will be seniors again."

"Do you think we'll still be close friends after we graduate? I mean, I know we'd always be friends, but do you think we will continue to hang out like we have been?"

"Of course! Why would you think anything would change?"

Craig put down his textbook, "Well, what if you and Johnny decide to move or need to spend more time together. Hell, you guys might even get married and adopt some babies or something. Sometimes relationships assist you in forgetting your friendships."

Sean rolled his eyes, "Who said anything about us getting married? It's only been two years since Johnny and I started dating and haven't treated you any differently than before, have I?"

"No."

"Then what makes you think it will happen after graduation? This is silly."

Craig smiled, "Forget I said anything. I'm sorry for being silly."

"Yeah," Sean chuckled.

Craig looked at Sean for a moment, but then noticed he was staring over his shoulder. The color left his face. Craig turned to see what got Sean so freaked and noticed Jaime approaching them with roses in his hand.

"Oh, I don't believe this shit!"

Jaime stood at the table staring at Sean and periodically glancing at Craig, "Hello Sean. Hello Craig."

"Eat me!" Craig told Jaime without even looking at him.

"Um, thanks for the invitation, but I'll pass."

"What the hell do you want, Jaime?" Sean asked.

"Well, I thought you and I could talk," Jaime glared in Craig's direction, "Alone, maybe?"

"Ha! Not going to happen!" Craig said.

"Craig..."

"I'm sorry, Sean, but there's no way in hell I'm leaving you alone with this ass douche!"

"Why don't you tell me how you feel?" Jaime sassed. To Craig, this was like waving a red flag in front of a bull.

Craig stood up to confronted Jaime, "You don't want me to tell you how I feel! Say something else smart to me!"

Sean stood up and reached over to grab Craig by the arm, "Craig, it's okay. Please..."

Craig unclenched his fists and sat back down while staring at Jaime with anger behind his eyes. "You want to talk to him; you are going to have to do it with me here!" Craig then addressed Sean, "I'm going to sit right here while he talks to you so please don't try to stop me."

Sean complied. Jaime rolled his eyes and sat down facing Sean trying to ignore Craig. He tried to give Sean the roses, but Craig smacked them out of his hand into the air landing across the table and on the floor, "You've got five minutes, so you better make it good!"

Sean tried to hold back laughing seeing Craig smack the flowers out of Jaime's hand and be serious, "What do you want, Jaime?"

"Well, I just wanted to apologize for the way I treated you. Those flowers were for you," Jaime mentioned looking across the table and on the floor.

"Apology years too late!"

"Craig!" Sean growled.

"Sorry."

"Jaime, there's no need for you to apologize or the flowers. It's over and forgotten. We've both moved on with our lives, remember? Why don't we just leave it at that? Is that it?" Sean went back to reading his textbook trying to ignore Jaime hoping he would just get up and go away.

"No, there's another reason why I wanted to talk to you."

Sean stopped reading and looked at Jaime. Jaime leaned into Sean as he backed up defensively. He then glanced in Craig's direction, "Does he have to be here?"

"Yes, he does! What do you want, Jaime?"

Jaime reached out to touch Sean's hand, but Craig smacked it. "Dude, what is your problem?" Jaime said sharply to Craig.

"How much time do you have?"

Jaime's attention was brought back to Sean, "I want you back."

Craig almost chocked on his own words, "Did he say what I think he just said?!"

"Are you out of your fucking mind?!" Sean said irritated.

Jaime moved his chair closer to Sean, "Sean, we belong together! I was wrong to have cheated on you. I was a fool to let you go. I want you to give me another chance because I'm still in love with you!"

"Bullshit!" Craig shouted.

"You were never in love with me, Jaime, remember? I don't even think you're capable of loving anyone else but yourself!"

Jaime falls out of the chair to his knees, "I've changed. I will become a better person because of you."

"I don't think you are capable of it! Look, I'm only going to say this once so listen carefully. There is no way in hell that I'm going to take you back! I don't even want us to be friends. I'm sorry if that sounds harsh, but too much has happened and too much can't be forgotten. There's nothing you can say or do to change that. I'm in love and I'm happy with a good man.... a real man. A man that treats me the way I deserve to be treated. Something you always fell short of doing. So, I'm sorry, but you come over here and the flowers were a big waste of time." Sean picked up his textbook and tried to get back to his studies.

"Sean, you don't mean what you are saying. I was your first love. You never forget your first.

Craig leaned across the table, "Do you have potatoes in your ears? The man has moved on so why you don't get the hint and get lost!"

Jaime looked at Craig and scoffed, "What do you know about our love?"

"You broke my heart, asshole! There is no love!" Sean yelled.

Everyone in the Student Union stopped what they were doing and looked at Sean's table. Sean got up, collected his textbooks, put them in his bag, and stormed out of the building. Jaime and Craig sat there for a moment before Jaime bent down to pick up the flowers from the floor. Craig tried to call out to Sean before he got too far, "Sean!" Students went back to doing what they were doing. Craig watched Jaime collect the flowers from the table and off the floor, "Well, I see you still know how to piss people off," Craig noticed one of Jaime's flowers on the floor and stepped on it. Jaime finished and started to leave.

"Where do you think you're going?" Craig asked.

Jaime scoffed, "Not that it's any of your business, but I'm going after him!"

"You take one more step in his direction and you and I are going to have words!" Craig threatened.

Jaime turned to Craig who was still sitting at the table, "You think I'm scared of you?"

Craig put his fists in the air, "I can give you two good reasons why you should be."

"What are you his bodyguard now?"

Craig got up from the table and walked over to Jaime. "No, I'm his friend. Something you would know nothing about. Stay away from him. I mean it. If you come around him again or upset him, they'll be no words. I'll break every bone in your body!"

Jaime had every reason to not take Craig's threats lightly considering Craig was several inches taller and a lot bigger muscle wise than him. With these factors in mind, it still didn't seem to bother him in the least.

"He will be mine again," he said with confidence in his voice.

Craig smirked and went back to the table to get his books, "Really? You seem damn sure of something that will never happen."

Jaime walked back over to the table, "Oh, but it will and you're going to make it happen."

Craig looked at Jaime, "Ha! Dream on!"

"Funny I know, but so very true."

"Not going to happen. Goodbye, Jaime!" Craig moved Jaime aside to leave.

"What would everyone think if they found out that you like to take it up the ass like the rest of us…. homosexuals? What would your beer-guzzling straight jock friends think? What would the sorority girls that you seduced after Friday night keg parties think? What would your cream cheese, country club parents think?"

Craig continued to leave as he gave Jaime the finger.

"What do you think Sean would say if he found out that you've been in love with him since sophomore year?"

Craig suddenly stopped. Jaime sat back down at the table, kicked his feet up, put the flowers down, and started tapping his fingers on the table. Craig came back to the table to confront Jaime, "Whatever you're thinking right now…"

Jaime smug demeanor terrified Craig, "Do I have your attention now? Good. Next time, you should be careful what you blurt out when you've had too much to drink. Now, sit your ass down!"

Craig did what he was instructed with a little tremble in his voice, "Jaime…"

Jaime leaned back and crossed his arms, "Don't worry, jock boy. Your secret will remain safe with me as long as you and I have an understanding."

"An understanding?"

"I want Sean back and you're going to help me make that happen. I want to know everything about Johnny and his relationship with Sean. I need information that can be useful. When he's mine, your secret will go back in the closet along with you!"

"He doesn't want you! Why can't you get that through your thick, empty head?"

Jaime slammed his hand on the table, "I don't give a shit what he wants! Just do it!" He proceeded to get up, walk around the table to Craig where he seductively moved his hands across Craig's chest, "Now, all this animosity and harsh words, can't we put this behind us and be friends?"

Feeling powerless, Craig allowed Jaime's hands to move down from his chest to his stomach, "Hell, we can even be friends... close friends...if you want." Craig finally removed his hands and turned his head with a disgusted look on his face. "I take it as a no. No worries...I've always been a fan of the big, strong, silent type. So, do we have a deal?" Craig reluctantly shook his head in agreement.

"Good!" Jaime picked up the flowers from the table and starts to leave.

"Why are you doing this? Why can't you just leave him alone?" Craig asked feeling deflated.

Jaime came back to Craig tapping the flowers against this chest, "Because I can!" He whispered.

"You haven't changed at all. You truly have a black soul."

"Ah, you flatter me so. Just make sure you tell me all that I need to know, and I'll make sure to keep my end of the bargain!"

"Why should I trust you?"

"Well, you don't have a choice here, do you?" Jaime smirked.

Craig thought for a moment and chuckled, "How do you expect to get Sean when he's with Johnny? I seriously doubt Johnny is going to give him up without a fight."

"Funny, shouldn't you be telling yourself the same thing? Besides, I took one relationship away from that breeder. What makes you think I can't do it again? Goodbye Craig!" Jaime walked out of the building as Craig sat back down at the table. Still trembling, he exhaled deeply and rested his head in the palm of his hands.

A Fine Evening

It was a movie night at Johnny and Seth's apartment. This was something Johnny had started two years ago and had become a monthly ritual ever since. The usual suspects were as follows: Johnny, Seth, Sean, David, Mark, and Craig. Each month, someone would be responsible for bringing the movies, someone would bring beverages and Johnny, or Seth would prepare or provide the snacks. They would watch movies, eat, drink beer, and have discussions in between, after, or even during the movie. The guys were used to Seth bringing over the worst movies possible while Mark brought artsy foreign movies. Craig usually brought movies that everyone seemed to enjoy watching.

Johnny sat in the armchair while Sean sat in between his legs on the floor. David and Mark sat on the floor leaning against the couch as Seth sat on one end of the couch and Craig on the other. They just finished one of the movies that Seth brought over. They were laughing as David took the movie out of the DVD player. "How could you say that movie was a classic?"

"What? It was released in 1986?" Seth said defending his choice.

Craig got up from the couch to stretch, "Just because it was released in 1986 doesn't make it a classic."

"Amen!" Johnny chimed in rubbing Sean's shoulders.

"Especially if it's *Howard the Duck*," Sean said as he leaned back into Johnny.

They laughed as Mark got up off the floor to stretch his legs. "Yeah, that was two hours of my life shot to hell."

"Alright, that's it! I'm no longer bringing over movies to movie night!"

"Promise?" Mark said.

Seth offended, "Fine if that's how you feel about it, but I'm letting you guys know now, no man on man love stuff! Craig and I don't need to see that shit!" Craig stood there silent but grinned forcefully in agreement.

"Not even kissing?" Mark said.

"Not even kissing, my friend!"

"Wait, so you would watch a woman kiss some freakishly-looking duck thing, but you won't watch two men kiss?"

Seth sat there and crossed his arms, "Sorry, but I have my limits."

Now, Mark squatted down and kissed David while Sean leaned his head back as Johnny began to kiss him. Craig stood there laughing at Seth feeling defeated, "Fuck you guys."

They laughed as Sean tried to get Seth's attention, "So, what are we watching next?"

"Another classic," Johnny mocked.

"Well, smart ass, it is a classic! *Alien*."

"Now that's better!" Craig said with a hint of excitement in his voice.

Mark got on his knees as he continued to be affectionate to David. Johnny and Sean playfully kissed one another as Craig stood by the dining room table, leaning against the chair staring at them. Seth felt his cell phone vibrate in his pocket, took it out to see who was calling. He walked out onto the balcony closing the door behind him to answer his call. Craig got tired of looking at Johnny and Sean kissing and went into the kitchen to grab another beer. After a few moments, Seth returned from the balcony, done with his call, sat back down on the couch. Johnny looked at him and smiled, "So, what's her name?"

"It was a guy."

"I knew it! We converted another one!" David laughed telling Mark.

"It was only a matter of time," Mark replied.

Seth grinned in amusement, "Shut up, you asses! It was Tagger."

Johnny stopped smiling and suddenly felt very nauseous. Seth laid the phone on the coffee table, "He's coming over to watch the movie with us. I told him we wouldn't start it till he got here. That's cool, right?"

"As long as he brings beer, any boyfriend of yours is a friend of ours," Mark joked.

Johnny cleared his throat and wiped his forehead, "Yes, of course, it's okay," Sean leaned his head back to ask Johnny, "Who is Tagger?" Johnny ran his finger through his hair, "He's our new lead singer." Sean closed his eyes enjoying Johnny's fingers massaging his scalp, "You didn't tell me you already found a new lead vocalist." Johnny continued to massage, "Yeah, this afternoon."

Seth leaned forward on the couch, "Sean, I'm telling you Tagger is good!"

Sean being the loving, supporting boyfriend added, "But not as good as Johnny." He grabbed his leg and hugged it.

Johnny's voice seemed shaky, "I need another beer. Be right back." He got up from the chair and stepped around Sean abruptly, "Hey, you okay? "Sean asked grabbing his calf before walking off.

"Yeah, I'm fine. Just need another beer." Johnny leaned down to kiss Sean on the forehead and went to the kitchen. Craig came out of the kitchen and returned to the couch with a fresh beer. Sean looked concerned but blew it off and got back into the conversation with Seth and the others.

"So, what's the story with this Tagger guy?" Sean asked Seth.

"Oh, he's cool. He has a great voice and stage presence. I think we made a really good choice."

"Well, you guys are amazing no matter who's singing. Yes, I'm a little bias when it comes to Johnny, but you guys put on one hell of a show the other night! When's your next gig?" David asked.

"We are playing The Pit two weeks from now. We start rehearsing a new show with Tagger tomorrow!"

"Well, we will be there! You guys' songs are great. The lyrics in your music seem to have a lot of meaning and feeling behind them, not very common nowadays." Mark added.

Johnny returned from the kitchen and noticed all eyes on him. Seth pointed to him, "You can thank that guy right there for that. He wrote every single one of them!"

"Wrote all of what?" Johnny asked.

"We were discussing how you write amazing songs for your amazing band and your amazing new singer!" Craig informed Johnny.

He took a sip of his beer and sat back down in the armchair that Sean was still leaning against. Once Johnny got comfortable, Sean repositioned himself between Johnny's legs resting his arms on his thighs, "I would like to think I had something to do with those amazing songs you guys love so much, inspiring the writer and all, but can't take credit for the new singer!"

"What does he sound like?" David asked Seth.

"He sounds somewhat like Johnny!"

Johnny sipped his beer faster trying everything possible to avoid eye contact with everyone in the room. He didn't want any more questions or remarks coming his way. Sean just kept rubbing his thighs which made it worse.

Mark asked, "Really? Is that true, Johnny?"

Sean looked up Johnny jokingly, "What, does he look like you too?" Johnny last swig of his beer must've gone down the wrong pipe because he began to cough.

Sean turned towards Johnny rubbing his arms, "Babe, you okay?"

"Yeah, are you alright?" Mark asked.

Johnny still coughing a little, "I'm fine, I'm fine."

The doorbell rang distracting all attention on Johnny at that moment. Sean got up to answer the door. He opened the door to see Tagger standing there with a 12 pack of beer.

"Hey, I'm Tagger. Is Seth here?"

"Hey, come on in. I'm Sean. Nice to meet you."

Tagger smiled and shook his hand as he entered the apartment. Seth greeted Tagger from the couch, "Tagger! What's going on, my man?"

Tagger walked over to Seth to greet him along with David, Mark, and Craig. Sean grabbed the beer from Tagger and took it into the kitchen to put it in the refrigerator. Johnny got up and walked over to Tagger to greet him, "Glad you could make it, man!"

"Thanks." Tagger shook his hand looking intensely into Johnny's eyes as if he was hypnotized, "I brought beer."

Johnny smiled, "Yeah, I noticed. Thanks. We're you able to find the place okay?" Johnny nervously chuckled, "Well, obviously since you are here…. now…. ahem…do you want a beer?"

"Can we start the movie now that the amazing Tagger is here?" Craig said sarcastically, "That would be an amazing thing!"

Johnny glanced at Craig annoyed as Tagger looked at him confused. "I'll grab you a beer, Tag. Are you hungry? We have some eats in the kitchen if you want anything." Johnny asked Tagger.

"Great." Tagger followed Johnny into the kitchen. Mark leaned back into David letting out a very loud, long belch. "Can you grab me one, too?"

"Well, that was very attractive, Mark," Sean said coming out of the kitchen. Johnny shortly returned from the kitchen, handed Mark another beer while grabbing Seth by the arm and taking him out to the balcony. He closed the sliding doors behind him. Sean looked at them wondering what was going on. Johnny looked as if he could strangle Seth, "Dude, what the hell?!"

"What?"

"You invited Tagger to movie night?!"

"So? What's wrong with that?"

"Are you insane? You invite someone who you said was flirting with me over to my apartment… that I share with my boyfriend! Do you think that was smart?"

Seth walked over to look out over the balcony and light a cigarette, "Will you calm down. Nothing is going to happen. You said yourself he was not flirting or interested in you. He is part of the band now. Thought it would be nice for him to hang out and get to know us."

Johnny paced the balcony with his hands on his head. "Hey! Do you see any other band members here other than you and me? The movie nights are for close friends and family. We just met this guy today!"

Seth exhaled, "I know, but he asked me this afternoon if he could come to watch movies with us. I didn't see the harm in it."

Johnny sighed, "This is not good. Not good at all."

"What are you freaking out about?"

Johnny walked over to Seth looking over the balcony, "I think you may have been right about Tagger flirting with me. I might have noticed something on our way to The Grill and in the kitchen just now, but I'm not completely sure."

"Oh shit…"

"Well, I could be wrong so let's just play it cool and see what happens."

Craig opened the sliding glass door a little frustrated, "Hey, would you to stop fucking around and come inside so we can finally start this movie?!"

Seth and Johnny came back into the apartment. Seth sat back down on the couch and looked at Tagger differently who was now sitting next to him. David and Mark were now lying across the floor in front of the television, Craig was sitting on the other side of Tagger and Johnny sat back in the chair where Sean repositioned himself again between his legs.

"Hey, you okay?" Sean asked. Johnny positioned himself in the chair to get comfortable, "Yeah, just talking to Seth about the playlist for tomorrow's rehearsal."

Sean was reassured and rested his head on Johnny's thigh as the movie started. David got up to turn off the lights. Johnny took a swig of his beer and noticed Tagger staring at him. Johnny, for a moment, couldn't help but stare back at him. Tagger smiled along with Johnny, but Johnny stopped when he noticed Seth looking at them. Johnny went back to watching the movie rubbing Sean's shoulders.

The Awful Truth

The next night, Sean and Johnny were lying in bed. Sean was lying on his stomach reading a book for school while Johnny leaned his head on Sean's back reading a Rolling Stone magazine. Sean put down the book, "Johnny, I need to tell you something."

"Yeah, what's up?"

"Ahem, I saw Jaime at school the other day."

Johnny put down the magazine and rubbed Sean's shoulders, "Did he say something to you?"

"He came up to Craig and me when we were studying and wanted to talk, to apologize for being a jerk."

"Was that all he wanted?" Johnny asked.

Sean hesitated, "Yeah, that's it."

Johnny wasn't quite buying it. He got up and sat back on his knees looking at Sean, "There's something you aren't telling me. Did he say something else to you?"

Sean exhaled and turned to face Johnny, "Do you remember the dream I've been having?"

"Yeah?"

"Well, I wasn't telling you the truth. It wasn't a dream about you being in an accident."

"Well, what was it about?"

"I'm standing in front of the mirror and bleeding from my wrists. The phone rings and I answer it. This hand touches my shoulder from behind and a voice says 'forgive me'..."

"Okay..."

Sean exhaled, "Well, I know I should've told you sooner, but didn't want you to see me as being weak. Johnny, the reason I'm telling you now about the dream is that when I saw Jaime, he wanted me to 'forgive him'......and get back together."

"Really..." Johnny said coldly.

Sean moved closer to Johnny, "Don't worry, I told him to go to hell because there was no way of us getting back together because I'm with you."

"So, you think the voice in your dream had something to do with Jaime?"

"I'm not sure but would make sense considering running into him the other day."

"Therefore, you couldn't tell me about this dream? This dream you've been having for a year now because you think it has something to do with your ex?"

"Yes, I didn't want you to get upset, but everyone told me that I should tell you."

"Everyone! You told everyone about this except for me?!" An angry Johnny got off the bed and walked over to the dresser to light some incense. "Why do you keep shit from me?"

Sean sat up, "What, this stupid dream?"

Johnny turned to Sean, "It's not a stupid dream if you've told everyone about it except for me! It must've meant something!"

Sean threw his hands up, "Well please save me some money on the psychologist and tell me what it means! I've been racking my brain all this time trying to figure this out, but if you have the answer in less than five minutes, please don't hold back! Please share with me!"

"It means that Jaime will always be a part of your life and an equation in our relationship. No matter how much I love you and no matter what I do, Jaime will always have some kind of hold over you that I guess I'll never understand."

Sean stood up, "Of course he will! He was my first boyfriend and my first love. He was a part of my life for a year!"

"The guy was an asshole to you! How can you still consider him a part of your life in any way?"

"Because he wasn't an asshole the entire time."

"The man broke your heart and you're bringing him into our relationship!" Johnny yelled.

"*This* is why I didn't want to tell you about the dream because of the way you are acting right now! I knew you would see it that way when this was nothing but a stupid dream!" Sean exhaled as he sat at the end of the bed.

Johnny exhaled, "You know, you've never been completely open about your relationship with him."

"That's not true."

Johnny walked over to Sean sitting on the bed, "Oh, really, then tell me about the relationship. No more secrets."

"I told you what it was like and you've met him. That should be all the explanation you need!"

"No! You were with this man for a year, but we've been together for two years! That should mean something to you! What is it with you and this guy?" Johnny inquired, "With such an impact he's having in your life, I know damn well that he wasn't an asshole to you the entire time! You don't seem like the type of guy that would tolerate that shit! Maybe you are who knows, with the shit you keep from me!"

Sean stood up in front of Johnny, "Oh, like you have been so open with me about your last relationship?"

"Hey! I told you everything about Natalie!" Johnny said defensively.

Sean sat back down, "What do you want from me?"

"I want and need for you to be more open with me and not run to our friends first when something is on your mind or bothering you."

"I don't like talking about Jaime or our relationship. It's in the past and I would like to keep it there."

"What's the big fucking deal? You had no problem talking about the break-up! You don't have a problem dreaming of him, but you have a difficult time talking about the actual relationship!"

"Fine!" Sean exhaled, "He was kind....at first, then he started to come home late. He stopped calling throughout the day and stopped returning my text messages. He became irritated with me. It was then I realized something was wrong. He acted like he didn't want me around anymore. I don't know why I stayed with him as long as I did. Maybe I didn't want to leave my comfort zone."

"Now I see why you were worried that I would see you as weak," Johnny said sarcastically, "I'm sorry, that was not called for, but Sean do you feel Jaime ever loved you?"

"Yes, I do, at first, but after that, I don't know what you would call it?"

"I would call it settling."

"What?" Sean said offended.

Johnny walked over to the bedroom window. He pulled the curtains enough to look out at the mountains and the skyline choosing his words carefully, "This is the man who treated you like shit, made you sad on every possible occasion and you think he loved you? I don't know what hold he had or has over you, but when are you going to finally let him go and let me in!"

"I don't know!" Sean yelled.

Johnny turned to Sean quickly. Sean got up from the bed and walked over to the window to Johnny. He noticed tears in Sean's eyes, "You better figure it out fast or...."

"Or what Johnny?"

Johnny took a deep breath, "This conversation is going nowhere. I can't talk about this anymore."

"Like it or not, he will always be in my heart in some way."

"Well, then it's obvious where that leaves me!" Johnny pushed Sean aside and stormed out of the bedroom into the living room. Sean followed him wiping his eyes, "Johnny!"

Johnny grabbed his guitar, book bag, and longboard, "I'm going to Seth's!"

"While you're there, why don't you ask yourself why you haven't told your parents about us yet?" Sean said angrily.

Johnny turned to Sean, "That's different and has *nothing* to do with what's going on here right now! Plus, you know how my parents can be!"

"No, actually I don't because I've never met them! I guess we all have our little secrets, huh, Johnny?!"

"Oh, fuck you!"

No, fuck you!" Johnny went to leave and grabbed his keys from the end table next to the couch. "Better yet, why don't you go and fuck Jaime! There's something you can dream about! Oh, and afterward, you can run and tell everyone about it...except me!"

"You're acting like a child, Johnny!"

Johnny stopped in the doorway and turned to Sean, "And you're acting like you don't have a boyfriend anymore! Mission accomplished!"

Johnny slammed the door behind him leaving Sean standing there in shock. He leaned against the wall and slid down to the floor. Sean realized for the first time in two years that he might be alone over this "stupid dream".

Two days and two very long nights later, Johnny was lying on Seth's couch watching television. During this time, he had not spoken to Sean but had watched Judge Judy episodes to know the law like the back of his hand. Seth walked out of his bedroom to see him flipping through channels, still in the same clothes he arrived in; a tank top and pajama bottoms.

"You know, if you call him, you'd accomplish more than making a permanent dent in my couch."

"I have nothing to say to him," Johnny said still flipping channels. Seth exhaled and sat next to him on the couch, "Johnny, I've known you for a long time and I know you are hurting. I also know that you love Sean more than you've loved anyone in your life, including Natalie, so you need to fix this!"

Johnny tossed the remote on the coffee table, "There's nothing to fix! The man keeps shit from me and he's dreaming about Jaime. For some reason, he won't let me in completely and the only thing I can think of is that he still wants Jaime!"

"Now you know that isn't true," Seth said, "You're just making all this up because your feelings are hurt right now. Call the man and tell him you overreacted, which you and I both know you did!"

Johnny pondered for a moment watching TV and then looked at Seth, "Did you know about the dream?"

"Huh?"

"Huh hell! Did you know about Sean's dream?!"

Seth hesitated, "He told me."

"You've known about this dream and didn't even tell me?"

"It wasn't my place to tell you, plus I thought you already knew!"

Johnny scoffed, "Think I'm overreacting?"

Seth looked at his watch and stood up as Johnny stretched back out on the couch, "Shit, I'm late. Listen, you need to call Sean and work this out! Nothing has happened that can't be fixed."

Johnny reached for the remote and started flipping channels again, "A little thing called trust and communication."

Seth stood in front of Johnny's view of the television, "The man didn't tell you about a dream he had. There's no crime there!"

Johnny pushed Seth aside, so he could finish watching television. "He's always going to put Jaime first in his life before me. There's always going to be something he's not telling me."

Seth snatched the remote out of Johnny's hand and hit him in the arm with it. "Johnny, regardless of what a horrible person he is, Jaime was the man's first love and boyfriend. Of course, he's going to be in his heart, but that doesn't mean that he's putting him first in his life! The man is crazy about you!"

Johnny continued lying on the couch, pouting, looking at the television. Seth noticed he wasn't getting through to Johnny, so he tossed the remote at him and walked to the door. As he turned the knob, he stopped, "Johnny, do you miss him?"

"I do..."

"Do you love him?"

"Yes..."

"Then call the man, dumbass! I'll see you at rehearsal tonight!" Seth left closing the door behind him.

Johnny continued to stare at the television but would glance over at his phone sitting on the coffee table. Hesitant, he reached over, grabbed his phone, dialed Sean's number, and waited for him to answer as the phone rang. He picked up after three rings, but it wasn't Sean. It was Jaime. "Hello?"

"Sean?"

Well, well, hi there little Johnny," Jaime said.

Johnny sat up very upset, "Jaime, why the fuck are you answering my boyfriend's phone? Where is he?"

"Boyfriend?" Jaime giggled, "I thought you two broke up. He's in the bedroom getting dressed. We're about to get dinner. I would've invited you along but thought might be a little uncomfortable since we're flying to Napa Valley for the weekend after dinner."

Johnny yelled, "Put Sean on the phone now!!"

"Why Johnny, you seem upset. Let me get Sean for you."

A few moments later Sean came to the phone, "Hello?"

Johnny at this point is beyond any rational thought, "Sean! What is going on? Are you with Jaime?"

"Johnny, I've realized that I'm still in love with him. I don't love you. We're over! I'm sorry. Forgive me…forgive me…forgive me… forgive me…forgive me…"

Johnny jumped up from the couch with a heavy gasp. That's the funny thing about dreams; they'll bite you in the ass when you least expect it. The television remote fell to the floor and he saw his cell phone in the same spot on the coffee table. He exhaled deeply still trying to control his breathing as he rubbed his eyes. He looked at the clock realizing that two hours had passed since Seth left for work. There was a knock at the door that startled Johnny. He hopped up from the couch to answer the door. When he opened the door, there was Tagger. Surprised, Johnny tried to compose himself, "Tagger. What are you doing here?"

"I'm sorry. Did I wake you?"

"No…guess I fell back asleep on the couch. Come on in."

Tagger entered the apartment and set his book bag and his longboard on the floor near the door. He walked in and stood in the middle of the living room examining the couch and looking at television, "Seth told me you were crashing here, so I wanted to stop by to see how you were doing."

Johnny walked by over to the couch and plopped back down into it, "I take it he told you what happened?"

"Yeah, he did," Tagger said nervously, "Are you okay?"

"Yes, I'm okay…considering."

Tagger sat on the other end of the couch, "So what are your plans for the day?"

"You're looking at it!" Johnny continued to flip through channels.

"Well, I have nothing to do today, maybe I'll join you."

Johnny shrugged, "It's a free country."

Tagger smiled and got a little more comfortable. He took off his flip flops and put his feet on the couch touching the soles of Johnny's feet already on the couch. Johnny noticed Tagger's toes wiggling against his soles, but didn't say anything and just continued watching TV to avoid an embarrassing situation, "Would you like a beer?" Johnny quickly got up from the couch and went into the kitchen.

Tagger also got up and walked over to his book bag near the door, unzipped it, and pulled out a bottle of liquor, "I have some whiskey!"

Johnny came out of the kitchen with a beer in each hand and saw Tagger squatting over by his bookbag rummaging through it with the bottle of whiskey on the floor. Tagger was wearing cargo shorts and a t-shirt that was a little smaller for his frame. Johnny noticed the surfboard tattoo on the lower left side on his back and that Tagger wasn't wearing underwear. Tagger found what he is looking for in his bag, which was his cigarettes. He zipped up his bag, stood up, and looked at Johnny with a smile. Johnny couldn't help but return a smile to him.

At Ally's apartment, Sean was sitting at the kitchen table as she was at the stove making tea. She gave Sean his cup of tea, took her cup, and sat on the kitchen facing Sean. He was picking through a bowl of chips on the table looking sad as Ally slowly sipped her tea, "Sean, it's been two days."

"I know," Sean sighed.

"Are you ever going to talk to him?"

"I don't know..."

"Please call him."

"I can't..."

"And why not?"

"Because he thinks that I'm keeping things from him. He thinks that I feel he's not important to me, that I don't take our relationship seriously."

Ally sipped, "Which is not true, right?"

"Of course, it's not true!" Sean finally found a chip that appealed to him and ate it. He blew on his tea and took a sip of his raspberry zinger, which was his favorite.

"But you told him about the dream?"

"Yes, and if I would've gone with my first instinct, we wouldn't be in this situation right now."

Ally grabbed a handful of chips from the bowl in front of Sean, "Why did you tell him Jaime was in the dream?"

"I didn't! I just thought that's what it was because of what Jaime said in the Student Union."

"You need to finally forget about Jaime. He's nothing but trouble!" Ally got up and went to the stove, grabbed the kettle, and poured more hot water into her tea.

"Well, that is easier said than done. I thought he was out of my life because I hadn't heard or seen him in years. Then suddenly, he shows up at school wanting me to forgive him and give him another chance."

Ally hopped back on the counter instead of sitting back down at the table, "Well, you have to do something to save your relationship with Johnny. You guys have something special that has been going on longer and stronger than what you and Jaime had. Don't lose that because it doesn't come around often and who knows if you'll find a love like that again."

Sean continues to play with the bowl of chips, "I think I might have already fucked things up with him."

"I'm not sure of that. He tends to blow up and jump to conclusions about things but feels bad about it later and apologizes. He will come around. Just give him time."

Sean turned in his chair to Ally, "How much time do I give him? It's only been two days and it feels like weeks!"

The doorbell rang, and Ally jumped off the counter running into the living room. Sean got excited to think that it might be Johnny. He sat up straight, adjusted his shirt, and fixed his hair; even checked his breath. As voices approached the kitchen, he realized one of them wasn't Johnny. Ally and Craig entered the kitchen.

Sean surprised, "Hey Craig, what are you doing here?"

"Um, I ran into Ally at The Green Apple yesterday and she told me what happened. She said you would be here, so I just wanted to stop by and see how you were doing."

"I'm hanging in there."

Craig addressed Sean with a nervous look on his face, "Could I talk to you for a minute in private?"

"Hey, you guys talk and I'm going to go over to Seamus'."

Sean got distracted momentarily by Ally's last words, "Whoa, whoa! Seamus? You two have been hanging out a lot lately. Might think you two are dating or something..." Sean laughed.

Ally moved quickly into the living room and grabbed her purse headed for the door avoiding all questions that might need answering. Sean and Craig followed out of the kitchen and caught her before she got out of the front door.

"Hold it, Lucy! You've got some explaining to do!" Sean said.

Ally stopped and looked at them, "We're seeing each other.... for a while now. Bye!"

Sean and Craig stood there for a moment in the living room in silence. Craig grinned at Sean, "I've seen them together. They look good...happy...good for them...must be love!"

Sean clapped his hands together, "So you wanted to talk. Let's go out of the balcony."

"Okay." Craig followed Sean out on the balcony. It was a beautiful clear day outside where you could hear the birds singing and the wind blowing through the trees. Craig and Sean were looking over the balcony embracing the beautiful scenery of West Burnsville.

"So, what did you want to talk to me about?"

"I'm gay." Craig blurted.

Sean turned to Craig with a shocked expression on his face, "You're what now?"

Craig continued looking out over the balcony unable to look at Sean, "You heard me."

"I think it warrants repeating."

Sean turned Craig to face him, "I said that I'm gay."

"Are you sure?"

"No, I just thought it would be the cool thing to say! Of course, I'm sure!"

"Well, you will have to excuse me, but this comes as a bit of a shock to me. I mean, have you always known?"

Craig exhaled, "Yes."

"What about all those girls you dated?"

"What can I say? I'm a damn good actor." Craig giggled.

Sean chuckled, "I'll notify the theatre department."

"I consider you my best friend, Sean, and I wanted to tell you before I told anyone else. I just felt it was about time for me to no longer keep this secret, finally be open to who I am."

Sean put his arm around Craig, "I think that's great! I truly admire you for doing that and I'm glad you felt comfortable enough to come and tell me. I'm here for you if you need me."

Craig changed the subject as he cleared his throat, "So, how are things with Johnny? Have you talked to him?"

"Not yet."

"Are you guys seriously no longer together?"

"I don't know, but as of right now, that's what it looks like."

Craig turned to Sean and gives him a big hug. "Whoa, what's this all about?" Sean asked.

"I just feel bad for you, but I'm here if you need me."

Still embraced, Sean started to feel a little uncomfortable with how tight Craig is holding him. Craig seemed to let loose a little allowing them to look at each other.

"Craig?" Sean whispered.

"Yes?" Craig said softly looking deep into Sean's eyes. Craig gently ran his hand through his hair, up and down the back of his scalp, allowing his fingers to glide across his ear. Sean was hesitant but allowed what was happening to happen. He moved in closer as Craig leaned into Sean and kissed him. They kissed for a few moments before Sean suddenly stopped and backed away, "I can't do this, I'm sorry," Sean said wiping his lips. Sean opened the patio doors and went inside into the kitchen. He got a glass of water while trying to catch his breath. His heart was racing as he noticed himself shaking trying to drink the glass of lukewarm water.

Craig entered the kitchen startling Sean. "I'm sorry. I don't know where that came from."

Sean exhaled deeply, "Why did you come out to me, Craig?"

"What do you mean?"

Sean turned to face Craig but at a distance, "That kiss out there! Is that the reason you came out to me? Or would it be because you found out that Johnny and I aren't together now?"

Craig tried to step closer to Sean, but Sean took a step back. "Yes, that is part of the reason, but the other reason is because that is who I am. You're my best friend and I felt it was important that you know."

Sean walked over to the kitchen table, pulled out the chair, and sat down, "You know, I'd always had a thing for you. I always felt there was a connection between us. I just figured we were such good friends and you were straight, I never thought it could be anything more, so I contained my feelings and thoughts for you. Then I met Jaime, and then Johnny and now…. that kiss. That kiss was something I'd thought of, but never knew would or could happen…. until now."

Craig pulled out one of the kitchen chairs and sat at the table, "So, what do we do now?"

"We do nothing! I love Johnny. I want Johnny. I need to work this out with him! We had a lapse in judgment and did something we've always wanted to do, but it can't happen again or mean anything. I'm sorry." Craig put his arms out on the table exhaling with disappointment.

Sean put his hand on Craig's forearm, "Craig, if things were different, if I was single at heart, I would be madly and completely in love with you, my best friend, but I've found the man I want to spend the rest of my life with and you will too. You're a great guy."

"How can you be so sure?"

"Because someone very kind and comforting told me the same thing once…and guess what, it did happen for me and it will happen for you."

What if you're the one for me? After four years, I don't think I could ever stop caring about you," Craig said deflated.

Sean smiled and moved his chair closer to Craig, "Good, I wouldn't want you to. I do love you as a friend, Craig. I'm just in love with Johnny."

"Do you think you could ever be in love with someone like me?" Craig said with tears in his eyes.

Sean patted Craig on the shoulder and got up from the table and walked over to the refrigerator. He looked at the pictures of Johnny and Ally, him, and Ally with Johnny, and him and Johnny, kissing and looking happy. Sean became very emotional as tears ran down his cheeks, "I don't know. I can't answer that."

Craig noticed something in Sean's voice and got up from the table. He walked over to Sean and put his hands on his shoulders as he slid his hands down his arms. "I know it's tough for you right now, but I'm here for you….as a friend."

Sean leaned into Craig, closed his eyes, and rested his head on Craig's chest, "I'm so glad you're here now. I need you."

Craig grabbed Sean, as his head fell back looking up in Craig's direction. Craig noticed his eyes still closed, but suddenly he opened them. He wiped the tears from Sean's eyes so softly and gently as if his hands were the tissues he needed. Craig leaned in to kiss Sean, but Sean hesitated. Craig continued to wipe Sean's tears while holding his face securely. After moments of staring into each other's eyes, Sean let his emotions take over and gave into Craig by kissing him.

After a few hours of whiskey and way too much beer, Tagger and Johnny were getting to know one another in a very intoxicated way. They were sitting on the floor in the living room, Indian style facing one another playing cards. Tagger poured another round of whiskey shots. They had decorated the floor around them with empty beer bottles.

"So, you didn't get the ring back?" Tagger laughed.

"Hell no, it was a cheap piece of shit…just like her!" Johnny laughed.

"So, let me get this straight, Sean's ex-boyfriend slept with your ex-girlfriend?"

Johnny laughed, "You got it!"

"Dude, that's fucked up!" Tagger laughed.

Johnny threw his arms in the air, "Welcome to my fucked-up life!"

Johnny grabbed a shot glass and downed a shot, "Seriously, Sean was there for me when things could've gotten really bad. He helped me stay on the right path and not get back into some really bad habits. I stopped playing my music which everyone seemed to think was the end of the world."

"Hey, that would be the end of the world. You're good!" Tagger said as he opened another beer, "So what are these bad habits of yours?"

Johnny pointed to the bottle of whiskey, "Well, you're looking at it," he then raised his bottle of beer at Tagger, "Drinking too much of this stuff, too. Beer, liquor, doesn't matter. It still does the same thing to me, get me drunk!"

"Amen to that. You want another beer?"

"What do you think?" Johnny said sarcastically.

Tagger got up and staggered into the kitchen returning with two cold beers, "So, if it weren't for Sean, you'd probably be in AA right now, huh?"

"Yeah, or worse…. could we talk about something else?" Johnny asked quietly as he finished off his beer.

"You miss him, don't you?"

Johnny opened his beer and took a swig, "Could we please talk about something else, please?"

"Okay, okay." Tagger opened his beer and took a swig, "So do you think you would date women again?"

Johnny smiled, "Is my sex life the main topic of conversation here?"

"What? I'm just getting to know you more," Tagger grinned.

Johnny took another swig of his beer and thought of something interesting to ask Tagger, "Let me ask you something, have you ever thought about dating guys?"

Tagger stopped grinning and took a swig of his beer avoiding eye contact with Johnny. Johnny thought he might have hit a nerve with Tagger or was finally getting to know the real Tagger, "No shit?" Johnny said intrigued.

"Yeah, well, I had this crush on a guy once about a year or so ago. I was at Midnights and he was singing this song called *Brand New Music*." While listening to Tagger, Johnny became extremely uncomfortable and began to sweat uncontrollably. "The song spoke to me as did the singer's voice. I felt I was in a trance. I couldn't take my eyes off him. He looked at me during one verse and for a moment I thought he was singing to me. It was then I realized I was in love."

Johnny seemed to have sobered up quick, "That's why you auditioned for the band, isn't it?"

"Yes."

"It was me, wasn't it?"

"It was always you, Johnny."

Johnny sat there puzzled, "You don't have a girlfriend, do you?"

"No, but I do have a very supportive sister. I wasn't sure how the other band members would react if they knew I preferred guys, well, one."

Johnny chuckled while he played with his beer bottle. "I'm flattered, but at the same time, should I be a little scared?"

"There's no need for you to be scared. I'm not psychotic. I'm not going to chop you up and put you in my freezer."

Johnny finished his beer, "Well, that is a relief because I would have to do some serious apologizing to Seth. Sorry, a little inside joke between Seth and I. Listen, Tag, I would be lying if I said I remember that night and remember looking at you, but to be honest, I wrote that song about Sean and our relationship."

"I figured." Tagger sighed.

"I don't know what's going on with us now, but I don't want to confuse you or lead you on."

Tagger moved over to Johnny, "Let me ask you something, Johnny, have you ever thought about me in that way?"

Johnny went into the kitchen to get another beer, "In what way?"

"You know, more than strangers, more than bandmates, more than friends?"

Johnny returned from the kitchen with a fresh beer and sat back down across from Tagger, "Again, I'd be lying if I said no, but I'm in love with Sean."

Tagger leaned in more to Johnny. Their knees were touching at this point as Tagger's hands were on Johnny's thighs.

"I don't want to get in between you and Sean," Tagger whispered.

Johnny looked deep into Tagger's eyes, but held him at arm's length, "That would be wise."

"Then what are we doing?"

Tagger moved Johnny's arm and got even closer. Closer to the point where their lips were touching, but Johnny jumped back, "We're drinking, we're getting to know one another, we're drinking…"

"You already said that," Tagger said softly with a grin.

"It needed repeating." Johnny again put Tagger at arm's length, "How's about we call it a night?"

Tagger exhales and moves back from Johnny. "I'm sorry. I shouldn't have done that."

"It's cool. We're drunk, and I know myself. I sometimes can't control my actions when I'm not working with a clear head." Johnny laughed.

"I know what you mean. I'm the same way."

They stood up, stumbled around some, and finally get their footing while laughing at one another.

"Thanks for hanging with me. It was fun and thank you for the whiskey." Johnny said. He opened his arms to hug Tagger. They fall into one another when they hug.

"No worries, my man. I had a good time." Tagger said. They stay embraced unmotivated to move from each other. They slowly came apart but didn't completely let go of one another. They played the staring game they've been playing since they first met, but this time when Tagger moved in to kiss Johnny, he kissed him back.

"You kiss like you sing," Tagger said softly.

Johnny smiled, "Good thing you sound like me." They continued to kiss standing amid empty beer bottles, an almost empty whiskey bottle and two shot glasses at their feet.

What Unfolds

Two days later, Tagger was reading a book on the park bench when he noticed a very well-dressed guy with sunglasses approaching him from the street. He looked up from his book to see Jaime standing in front of him. He scooted over to make room on the bench. Jaime sat down, removed his sunglasses, and stared at Tagger. Tagger closed the book on his lap as Jaime continued to look at Tagger intensely, "Well?" Jaime said.

Tagger lit a cigarette and grinned, "It worked."

Jaime clapped his hands with a big grin on his face, "See, I knew it would work! Now, you just have to remember to stick to the rest of the plan."

"Explain to me again why I'm doing this?"

"I need Johnny out of the picture, so I can get Sean back. Now, you just keep doing what you're being paid to do, and I'll take care of the rest."

"But I don't want Johnny...I thought you and I were going to get together."

"Look, I told you that you're not my type...you're cute and all, but kind of stupid. I want my ex back. So, you just continue to pursue Johnny and break up their relationship and I'll keep paying you."

"Ok, well, I got in the band, used the information you gave me about the song, seduced him, so the rest should be pretty easy, but I have to tell you, he seems serious about Sean."

"He kissed you, didn't he?" Jaime asked.

"Yes, just like you said he would. You were right about the whiskey!"

"Now that you have the fires going, you need to bring up the heat!"

"Well, what's next?"

"Get Johnny! I want him completely out of the picture!"

"Ugh, good thing you're paying me, but do I want the band." Just then, Jaime put an envelope of cash on Tagger's lap and shrugged, "Then take the band! Just make sure Johnny's out of my way and out of the picture! I want Sean!"

Tagger took the envelope and put it in between the pages of the book. Jaime got up to leave when Tagger said, "How am I supposed to get the band from Johnny and Seth?"

Jaime turned around aggravated, "Dude, do I have to do everything for you? You're an actor! Use your imagination…use your skills…and make sure it's convincing or I'll drop you off at the corner I picked you up on, and then you can continue to whore yourself to the highest bidder! I gave you the information, the resources, and the cash. You were hired you to do a job so do it! Now, stop asking so many questions and get Johnny away from Sean! If you want the band bad enough, figure it out for yourself!" Jaime put on his sunglasses and walked back to his BMW. Tagger sat there for a moment before starting to count the money in the envelope.

After two weeks, Johnny finally got up from Seth's couch and moved back home, unfortunately, Sean was still living on Ally's couch. They tried talking things through, but Johnny's anger still got the best of him, so they decided it would be best if they spent some more time apart. Johnny sat at the dining room table, drinking a cup of coffee with his feet propped up on the chair reading the newspaper. The doorbell rang and he put down the paper to get the door. Johnny opened the door to see David.

"Dave! What's going on, man?!"

"Hey, I've got some great news! May I come in?"

"Yeah, what's the news?" David came into the apartment and sat down on the couch. Johnny sat down in the armchair as David looked around, "Have you talked to Sean?"

"No."

"When is all of this going to be over?"

"We just decided we needed some more time apart. Well, it's more he wants to talk and work it out and I'm still too angry to listen so…"

"Well, I hope you guys can work this out."

Johnny changed the subject, "So, what's the big news?" David began to smile from ear to ear, "Mark and I are getting married!"

"Holy shit, that's great! Congratulations!" Johnny got up and moved over to David giving him a big hug.

"Well, I wanted to tell you and Sean together, but I told him this morning and wanted to tell you as soon as possible. We're having an engagement party at Midnights on Saturday. I would like for you to be there."

"You talked to Sean this morning?"

"Yes."

Johnny cleared his throat, "How is he?"

"Why don't you go ask him for yourself?" David smiled.

Johnny smirked and changed the subject, "I'll tell you what, I'll check our schedule and if we're free, the band will play your party free of charge!"

"Thank you so much, man. I appreciate this. This is the best present you could've given us. Well, there's one more present you could give us, and it will not cost you a thing!"

"What's that?"

"Come to the party with Sean. It would mean so much to us if we saw you guys their arm in arm again."

"Let me ask you something, while you were upstairs, did you mention this to him?"

"Yeah, I did."

"And what did he say?"

"He said it was up to you."

"Well, I'm just not ready yet. I'm sorry. I know he's family and you're just looking out for him, but just let us work this out for ourselves, okay?"

"I'm not just looking out for him and I'm a little offended that you would think that." Before Johnny could respond, there was a knock at the door. Johnny got up and answered the door to see Tagger standing there. Johnny became nervous, "Hey…Tag…what's up?" Tagger gave Johnny a hug and a kiss on the lips. David noticed the affection given to Johnny from Tagger and stood up from the couch.

Tagger came into the apartment and noticed David standing there. "Oh, I'm sorry. I didn't know you had company…"

Johnny closed the door, "Tag, you remember Dave, Sean's cousin."

"Oh yes, how are you?" Tagger reached out to shake David's hand, but David ignored Tagger's gesture. "Well, I now see what's keeping you from going downstairs." David stormed off into the kitchen. Johnny followed David, "I'll be right back," Johnny told Tagger standing in the living room feeling very out of place. Johnny walked into the kitchen to find David leaning against the counter, arms crossed, waiting for Johnny to enter the kitchen.

"Dave, I know what you're thinking, but let me explain."

"Yeah, you need to explain to me why that guy was kissing you when you're involved with my cousin?"

"It's been two weeks and we don't know what's going on with us! Frankly, I'm just not ready to make things all cozy again, plus Tagger's just a friend. We're bandmates."

"Well, the last time I checked, friends don't kiss each other on the lips!"

"I do remember that's how your cousin and I started dating in the first place," Johnny realized that might not have been the best example to give David, "Forget I said that, but you know what I mean."

David exhaled, "What's going on here, seriously?"

Johnny walked over to the cabinet behind David, grabbed two coffee cups, and poured himself and David a cup of coffee. Johnny handed David a cup and sat down at the kitchen table. Johnny took his cup and sat down.

"Start talking!" David told Johnny.

Johnny took a sip of his coffee and sighed, "Sean told me about his dream. The real one he had been having for over a year. He finally decided to tell me the truth weeks ago when everyone else knew way before then. I take it you knew as well?" Johnny looked at David as he nodded in acknowledgment, "He said the dream had to do with Jaime, whom he saw on campus recently. Well, there was a voice in the dream telling him to forgive him and when he saw Jaime on campus, he asked Sean the same thing."

"You and I know there is no way Sean would get back with Jaime."

"I know that, but I don't want Jaime in our life anymore. I want Sean to put me first in his life and finally let Jaime go!"

"What makes you think he hasn't? Johnny, you must realize that Sean loved Jaime just like you loved Natalie, and just because she hurt you doesn't mean that she's still not in your heart in some way. You loved that girl for three years of your life. She will always have a place in your heart, just like Jaime will have in Sean's. Sean's not trying to replace you or put that asshole first before you, he's just trying to understand a dream that sounds more like a nightmare. Sean's in love with you and you love him. Work this out."

Johnny sat there and listened to what David had to say. He realized that he might have taken this a little too far and it was time to stop being angry and to start talking to the man he loved.

At that moment, Tagger came into the kitchen, "I'm sorry to interrupt, but I wanted to tell you that I'm leaving, Johnny."

"No, you can stay. I have to go anyway," David got up from the table and put his coffee cup on the counter. "Thank you for the coffee. I'll call you later about next Saturday."

"You still want us to play?" Johnny asked.

"Yeah, I do," David sighed, "I'll call you later." Johnny got up and hugged David. David whispered in Johnny's ear, "Work it out, please, for me." Johnny closed his eyes and squeezed tighter. David left without acknowledging Tagger. Johnny and Tagger were now alone in the kitchen as well as the apartment. Johnny got up from the table and hopped up on the counter staring at the floor. Tagger tiptoed over to Johnny with his arms behind this back, "He doesn't like me."

"What do you expect? You were kissing the guy his cousin is dating." Johnny said in a low tone.

Tagger stood in between Johnny's legs casually putting his hands-on Johnny's thighs, "Well, if I remember right, we've done more than just kiss."

Johnny moved his hands away, "Your memory is bad because all we did was kiss!"

"Well, a guy can hope, can he?" Tagger playfully put his hands back on Johnny's thighs.

Johnny aggressively pushed Tagger back, "He's still my boyfriend, Tag!" Tagger stood there puzzled, "Then what do you call what has been happening between us for the past two weeks?"

Johnny looked at Tagger seriously, "Nothing happened! We kissed and that was it. Nothing more! I'm sorry, the kiss was a drunken distraction."

"You were playing me?" Tagger said with anger.

"There was no playing here, Tag! You were acting out a fantasy you've always had about me, and I was indulging in some very bad self-destructive behavior in which I regret!"

"This was *not* a fantasy! I love you!" Tagger yelled.

"You don't love me. You love my music and what it represents."

Tagger pulled out the chair from the kitchen table and plopped down in it, "I thought that was you. I thought falling in love with your music was falling in love with you."

"You were wrong. There's more to me than the words I write and sing."

"Really, what's that?"

"Sean. He completes me. He's everything I want and need in a person. I love him and always will."

Tagger got up and stormed into the living room. Johnny followed as Tagger turned back to see Johnny standing in the living room, "And by the way, my name is Tagger...asshole!" Tagger slammed the door as he left. Johnny exhaled with relief and with a smile, Johnny jumped around with excitement and ran into the bathroom to take a shower, but before he could get the water running hot, his cell phone rang. Johnny answered it and got some unexpected news from New York that would have to put his current plans on hold.

Later that night at Craig's place, he and Sean were having dinner and watching old movies on the floor in the living room. They had ordered a pizza with a couple of beers. Sean hadn't heard from Johnny and was spending most of his free time with Craig. Even though they were watching a movie, they continued to be engrossed in conversation and laughter ignoring Bette Davis on the screen.

Sean finished his third piece of pizza and second beer, "Thanks for dinner. It was great!" Sean said wiping his mouth.

"Yeah, who knew pizza and beer could be so good." Craig laughed.

Sean kept looking at his phone to see if he had received a text message or a missed call. Craig had noticed Sean doing this throughout the night, "He hasn't texted or called you, has he?"

"No." Sean sighed deeply.

"Don't worry, he will," Craig rubbed his hand between Sean's shoulder blades as Sean looked at him and smiled, "You think so? I didn't fuck it up, did I?"

"I don't think so, but I will tell you this, it is good to see you smile and laugh even though you are going through a difficult time right now."

"Well, thanks to you." Sean sat there as Craig collected the plates and bottles and took them in the kitchen. Sean got sad for a moment because he realized how much he missed watching movies, eating take-out, and drinking beer with Johnny on the floor of their living room. Craig came back from the kitchen to see Sean looking sad, "Hey, are you okay?"

"I think I need some air," Sean said shaken.

Sean got up from the floor and went out to the porch. Craig opened the door to see Sean crying and talking to himself as he paced on the porch.

"You sure you're okay?" Craig asked.

Sean talking to himself, "What the hell am I doing? I'm having dinner, great conversation, and giggling like a schoolgirl with another man! A hot ass man who's supposed to be my best friend… who I kissed and is not my boyfriend because I already have a boyfriend… but that boyfriend doesn't want to talk to me because he is angry with me for keeping a dream from him about my ex-boyfriend…which I should have told him about in the first place… but told everyone else but he and all I want is for him to call me or text me or something because I love him and want him back and….."

"Sean?"

Sean continued pacing, talking to himself, "I mean, technically I haven't cheated on him since we haven't had sex, but we have kissed, I mean that is not cheating, right?" Sean stopped and looked at Craig, "I'm cheating, aren't I?"

"Sean…"

"Craig! Johnny and I haven't officially broken up, which makes us still boyfriends…. I think."

"I know, Sean."

"Then what are we doing here?"

Craig held Sean's arms firmly, so he would stop being fidgety and looked him in the face, "I'm not trying to take Johnny's place. I'm just trying to make you happy. Seeing you down these past few weeks, I just wanted to cheer you up. That's just what friends do! And as far as the kiss goes, it was just a kiss. A good kiss, but that's it, just a kiss."

They smiled and chuckled, "See that is what I like to see. I just want to make sure it remains on that beautiful face of yours!" Craig said.

Sean seemed to calm down and relax, "Why do you always know the right things to say?"

"I've had plenty of practice dating women." Craig joked.

"Oh, is that how you see me as a woman?"

"A very hairy and handsome one."

Sean hugged Craig. Just then they heard some jazz music coming from the open window of Craig's next-door neighbor. "You hear that? Craig said.

"Yeah, sounds great," Sean said looking around. "It sounds like your neighbors are having a romantic evening." Craig and Sean were still embraced, "Do you know what I would like to do with you right now?"

"What?" Sean responded.

"Will you dance with me?"

Sean looked at Craig and knew it was too hard to say no to someone that has been such a good friend to him. He felt an innocent dance would not harm anyone, so Sean said, "Yes."

They slowed danced on the porch as the music from the neighbors continued to play. Sean rested his head on Craig's chest and he closed his eyes. He couldn't help but imagine if this were Johnny what a perfect night it would be. He started to become emotional again, hoping and praying that Johnny would contact him, but here in Craig's arms, for the moment, he felt safe and loved even though it was the wrong guy. So, Sean just swayed to the music and let the mood take over him, for tonight. They danced until they heard the music end. They stopped dancing and quietly looked at one another.

"Stay with me tonight," Craig whispered.

Sean's first instinct was to say no, that he should be heading home to call Johnny, but he didn't go with his first instinct, he went with his first emotion, "Yes."

Craig was shocked yet happy, "Are you sure?"

"No, but I want to stay." Sean smiled.

Craig and Sean slowly moved into one another and kissed with caution, then that caution was replaced with passion with a little bit of sexual tension. They continued to kiss as they moved back into the house, stumbled through the living room, and into Craig's bedroom. Craig laid Sean on the bed and began kissing his neck and ear. Sean took off Craig's shirt which revealed his strong, muscular physique. Sean wrapped his fingers around Craig's triceps then slid his hands easily down the sides of his torso. Craig removed Sean's shirt as he began to kiss and fondle his chest and nipples. Sean moaned with ecstasy falling completely under Craig's spell.

The light coming from outside danced on the windblown curtains of the open window. Sean unzipped Craig's pants and pulled them down past his amazing round butt exposing his grey boxer briefs. Craig proceeded to do the same thing to Sean as his body arched as he let out a passionate moan. Craig kissed down his chest to his crotch where he stayed for the next fifteen minutes. With Craig's face buried in Sean's crotch, he reached around with his big hands, pulled off Sean's pants, and squeezed his ass which made Sean moan louder giving the neighbors some music of their own.

Happy Days

It was Saturday, the night of David and Mark's engagement party at Midnights. All of Mark and David's friends and family were there. Johnny made it back in time from New York to attend the party. Sean had not arrived, yet which was making David very nervous.

The lounge was decorated with twinkle lights and candles and streamers courtesy of Michelle and Ally. The band sounded great, even though Johnny wasn't playing. Seth decided to play lead guitar in Johnny's place. There was a long table alongside the stage with a maroon tablecloth with a candle and yellow roses with reddish maroon accent centerpieces that were breathtaking. There were bottles of champagne distributed at certain spots in the center of the table. David and Mark sat on one side of the table surrounded by friends and family mingling amongst each other.

Michelle stood up and tapped the side of her champagne flute with her fork, "I would like to make a toast."

Everyone stopped talking and looked at Michelle. The band was on a break and it got quiet in the lounge with no other patrons around since it was a private party.

"On this very special occasion, I would like to wish two very special friends of mine, Dave, and Mark, all the happiness and love in the world. Congratulations!" Everyone raised their glasses to the couple and wished them congratulations. Dave and Mark toasted their glasses and kissed. Mark looked very happy, but David still looked worried since Sean hadn't arrived. After taking a sip from his drink, David got his phone from his pocket to see if he had any missed calls. David excused himself and snuck away to call Sean. Mark followed David outside to make sure everything was okay. David was sitting at one of the outside tables playing with his cell phone.

"Hey, everything okay?" Mark asked.

"I'm just worried about Sean. He should have been here by now."

"He'll be here. Just running late that's all."

Mark put his arm around Dave when Michelle came outside abruptly white as a ghost. They looked at her, "What's wrong with you?" David asked.

"You guys should get in here. You're not going to believe this!"

David and Mark rushed inside with Michelle and stood there in shock along with the rest of the party guests to see Tagger serenading Johnny with the song Johnny wrote for Sean, *Brand New Music*. After Tagger finished, there was a round of very awkward applause. Tagger blew Johnny a kiss which Johnny tried to ignore.

Ally, who was sitting across from Johnny, looked past him to see Sean and Craig standing at the door with gifts in their hands. Johnny noticed Ally looking past him and turned around the see them. Johnny got up from the table, walked between Sean and Craig, glancing at Sean as he pushed opens the door to leave. Sean handed Craig the gift he was holding and followed him outside. Now Craig realized that everyone was looking at him including the happy couple and Michelle. Tagger lit a cigarette, exhaled, and smirked with satisfaction.

Johnny was leaning on the wall smoking a cigarette. He noticed that Sean was walking towards him but didn't make eye contact. Sean walked in front of him trying to get his attention but ended up walking into his smoke. Sean sat down on a chair next to the wall. There was a moment of silence before Johnny said anything to Sean, "How long have you been here?"

"Long enough," Sean exhaled.

"So, you heard that in there?"

"Oh, I heard enough…"

"Are you okay?"

"I don't think so. That was the song you wrote for me…"

"I know. I think I'm going to be sick."

"That makes two of us!"

Sean noticed part of Johnny's metallic blue button-down shirt was tucked into his pants and pulled it out to make it look the way it should. Johnny didn't move, just let Sean do it as if it were natural, "I see you're smoking again."

Johnny scoffed, "Do you blame me?"

"I guess not." Sean sat against the brick building.

Johnny put out the cigarette and squatted next to Sean, "I'm sorry… I miss you."

"You do?"

"Yes, I just want all of this to be over. I'm not angry anymore, Sean. I want you to come home."

"Why haven't I heard from you, a text message or phone call in days? Weeks?"

"I had to go to New York for a family emergency. I was going to come over to Ally's to talk to you when I got the phone call. I got on the first plane to New York. I did want to call you and text you, but my emotions were all over the place and didn't want to start another fight with you. I wanted to talk to you with a clear and calm head. I know I should've called, I'm sorry. Forgive me?"

"What?" Sean said to Johnny with a shocked expression on his face as his dream reappeared in his mind, "I said do you forgive me for not calling or texting?"

"What about Tagger?"

"What about him?"

"It sounds like there's much more going on than just music playing."

"Nothing is going on between us."

Sean stood up and walked over to the curb between two parked cars. "What about him kissing you?"

"Dave told you that."

Sean turned back to Johnny, "Yes he did. Did you like kissing him?"

"Tagger kissed me, and it didn't mean anything!"

"The man was singing *our* song to *you*!!"

"Yeah, I know. I was there, remember?!!"

"Did you like it, Johnny!?"

"Like what?"

"His kiss…"

Johnny interrupted, "No!"

"It only happened that one time?" Sean asked.

"No…"

"When was the other time?" Sean walked back over to Johnny and squatted in front of him balancing himself by putting his hands on Johnny's knees.

"After we fought, Tagger came over, we were drinking and then we kissed. It shouldn't have happened, and I regret it. I'm so sorry."

"Well, at least it took several attempts before you decided you didn't like kissing him," Sean said as he stood up in front of Johnny.

Johnny dropped to his knees looking up at Sean, "It meant nothing! Sean, I love you! I'm still in love with you. I wasn't thinking, and it will never happen again." Sean looked down into Johnny's eyes as he ran his fingers through Johnny's hair. Johnny wrapped his arms around Sean's waist and held him tightly. Johnny began to cry, "I don't want him. I want you! I want to work through this and move forward. I didn't mean to hurt you because I know you would never do anything like that to hurt me. Please forgive me. It was just a stupid kiss that meant nothing! I'm so sorry, baby!"

"I think there's something you should know before you ask for my forgiveness…"

Johnny cried into Sean's pelvis being comforted by Sean's hands. "I slept with Craig." Johnny stopped sobbing and slowly let go of Sean, "You what?"

"I slept with Craig."

Johnny stood up and wiped his eyes, "Are you serious?"

Sean took several steps back from Johnny, "I'm sorry."

"How could you do that?"

"I hadn't heard from you and Craig was there for me when I was feeling like shit."

Sean tried to come close to Johnny again, but Johnny stepped away, "So that gave you the right to fuck him?"

"Johnny, I'm sorry. It was a moment of weakness. It just happened once and never again."

Johnny put his arms over his head and began to pace with anger, "I can't believe you did this to me... to us! I mean, what were you thinking? Yes, I kissed Tagger, but I didn't fuck him."

"Johnny, neither one of us is proud of what we've done," Sean said trying to reason with Johnny. "But we can get past this and move forward, right?"

"No! What you did was so much worse! You fucked him!" Johnny yelled.

"You kissed Tagger! It's still unfaithfulness!"

Johnny stopped pacing and looked at Sean long enough to notice tears building up in Sean's eyes.

"Johnny, we need to forgive one another. You have to forgive me as I have forgiven you." Sean cried.

"I don't have to do shit!" Johnny shouted. "We're over! Come get your shit *out* of the apartment! I never want to see you again!"

Johnny stormed off sobbing back to the entrance of the bar. Sean cried out to him unable to move, "Johnny! Don't do this. It isn't fair."

Johnny stopped and pointed at Sean, "Fuck you and fuck what's fair!" Ally came outside to find out what was keeping Sean and Johnny when Johnny walked past her almost knocking her over entering the bar. "Johnny?" Sean stood there in the middle of the sidewalk sobbing loudly as Ally ran to comfort him.

A week later, the guys met David and Mark at the tuxedo shop to get fitted for their tuxedos. Johnny, Sean, Seth, and Craig were in the waiting room while Mark and David were getting fitted. The tension in the waiting room was so thick you could cut it with a knife. Johnny and Sean sat on opposite sides of the room where Craig sat next to Sean who was reading a magazine. Sean had come by the apartment when Johnny was at rehearsals or working to get his belongings and moved in with Craig. Craig had set Sean up in the spare bedroom. A very tough transition for Sean, he seemed to deal with the breakup and departure from his home well. Johnny kept looking at his watch and sighing with frustration.

Sean saw that Johnny was impatient about something, "Are you okay?"

Johnny sighed with irritation, "If you must know, I have rehearsal and running late."

"I'm sorry for being concerned..."

"There's no need for you to be concerned about anything that involves me anymore!"

Sean sighed and put the magazine back on the table. Johnny noticed that Sean's forearm was touching Craig's forearm on the chair beside him.

Johnny leaned forward in Sean's direction, "Shouldn't you be swimming, doing something athletic with your gay stereotype over there?"

"Johnny..." Seth said reading a magazine.

Sean leaned forward towards Johnny, "How about we get some booze and see how many guys we can kiss? Boy, doesn't that sound like ginger-peachy fun?"

"Sean…" Mark said as the tailor was getting his pants measured. David was trying on his jacket, getting it sized by the tailor's assistant.

Johnny stood up, "How about someone tell Sean a secret so he can keep something else from me!" Johnny walked over to Sean and leaned down to him bracing himself on the arms of the chair, "Then afterward, you can have sex with your empty-headed jock!"

Offended, Craig stood up and approached Johnny, "What's your problem, man?"

Johnny stood up, "If you know what's good for you, you would back the *fuck* away from me!!"

Seth came in between them holding Johnny back. Johnny's right arm was flexed and ready to swing at Craig. Sean got up and stood in front of Craig.

Dave walked out from the dressing room to the waiting area, "If you guys are going to fight and bicker the entire time, do it someplace else…not here, and not at our wedding!"

Johnny pushed Seth off of him and fixed his clothes, "I'll do you one even better… find yourself another groomsman! I'm out of here!"

"Johnny, wait!" Mark called out.

"Let him go. Just let him go." Sean sighed.

Seth scoffed at Sean, "Yeah, which was easy for you to do, wasn't it?"

Just outside the shop, Jaime was looking into the window. He ducked behind some bushes when Johnny came storming out. Jaime watched as Johnny walked down the street. When he was out of sight, Jaime took out his cell phone and dialed a number. He waited for the person on the other end to answer. "Hey, it's me. Listen, do it tonight! I'm tired of waiting for Tagger. Make sure you do it right and do it well. I don't want anything to stand in my way from getting back with Sean. No, just do what you must do, but make sure it's random. I don't want this to come back on me. Yes, hurt him good…take care of Tagger too! I don't want any loose ends…" Jaime hung up the phone and with his trademark smirk walked away from the store.

At Midnights later that afternoon, Johnny stormed through the door to join the rest of the band, minus Seth, to rehearse. When he got there, he noticed the band already rehearsing, but they were rehearsing material that Johnny's never heard of before. He stood there, listened for a few moments before the band even noticed him, and stopped playing. Johnny walked towards the stage, "What the hell was that?"

Tagger put down the microphone, hopped down from the stage and met Johnny halfway, "Well, I figured since you would be busy with the wedding…"

"You decide to rehearse music other than what I wrote?!"

"Well, your songs have been somewhat on the depressing side lately, don't you think?"

"Meaning?" Johnny said as he crossed his arms.

Tagger smirked, "Well, I mean since you and Sean are over…."

Johnny interrupted, "Listen to me, I don't know what kind of game you're playing, but this is my band! I write the songs, I say what's going to be sung and what's going to be played, you got it?! You've only been here a minute and can be replaced just like that!"

Tagger chuckled and shook his head, "I don't think so, Johnny. See, since you have been dealing with your gay drama for the past couple of weeks, I am the one that has kept this band together. I'm the one writing material that the other members find…. refreshing and new. They also agree that the band should make some changes and move in a different direction…for the better."

Johnny started to grind his teeth, "You son of a bitch. You think you will get away with this?"

Tagger put his hand on Johnny's shoulder, "Baby, I already have. Look, there are no hard feelings here. We just feel you should allow someone else to step in and express a new sound, a new voice, brand new music," he smirked.

"I advise you to remove your hand if you want to keep it!" Johnny said as Tagger removed his hand.

Johnny moved away from Tagger and walked up to the other band members, "Is that how you all feel?! Is this what you all want?! You want me out?! HUH?!"

The other band members looked around not saying anything or looking at Johnny. Tagger looked at Johnny and grinned with pleasure. Johnny stepped back from the stage slowly feeling betrayed by his band; guys whom he thought were his friends. He then turned to Tagger, "Alright, you win! I'm out! I guess you got what you wanted!"

Johnny attempted to leave when Tagger grabbed his shoulder and turned him around, "Johnny, it's what's good for the band. I'm good for the band now."

Johnny laughed, "You don't know shit!"

"Well, I'm you now. That I know," Tagger grinned.

Johnny stood there for a moment looking at Tagger with a cold stare in his eyes.

"Oh, now come on. Don't let this set back come between us." Tagger said, "We can still make beautiful music together," Tagger ran his fingertips down Johnny's chest. He smiled with a slight flirtation in his eyes, turned to leave, then came back with a right hook to Tagger's face. He fell to the ground like a sack of potatoes taking out some chairs and a bar table.

Johnny shook his hand, "No, you are better solo." After Johnny left, the band members ran to aid Tagger who laid on the floor out cold.

Hours later, Mark met Johnny at Flannigan's Pub in West Burnsville. They have many empty pint glasses in front of them and it didn't look like there were signs of stopping. Johnny lit another cigarette and looked around them. There were two other patrons at the end of the bar and a middle-aged, slightly intoxicated, couple dancing between the bar tables to classic rock coming from the jukebox in the corner of the bar.

"You hit him?" Mark said.

"Out like a light. I have the bruised hand to prove it," Johnny showed Mark his bruised knuckles. The bartender took some of the empty glasses away.

"So, no more band?" Mark asked Johnny, "You're just going to let Tagger get away with this? It's your band! You and Seth started this band!"

"There's nothing I can do now. The other members made up their minds. Tagger's in and I'm out."

"How does Seth feel about this?"

"I don't think he knows. He never made it to rehearsal after getting fitted for his tuxedo."

"You think he will stay with the band?"

"I doubt it," Johnny sighed and put out his cigarette, "Come on, let's get out of here." Johnny and Mark got up from the bar stools, pushed them in, and said goodbye to the bartender.

"I'm buying you guys two more drafts," the bartender said. Johnny and Mark looked at one another, pulled out the stools, and sat back down. Johnny lit another cigarette as two more drafts were placed in front of them.

Mark took a sip of his beer, "So what are you going to do?"

"I have no idea," Johnny exhaled and took a sip of his beer as well. Mark played with his beer mug, "Maybe you and Seth can start another band? You know he will be there for you no matter what, plus it was your music that got the band where it is in the first place. What's to say you can't do it again? Hell, even better this time!"

Johnny smiled at Mark, "Yeah, you're right. Thank you."

"It's my pleasure."

"Listen, I'm sorry for my behavior at the shop. I didn't mean to act all crazy psycho. Please let Dave know I would like to be a part of the wedding," Johnny said.

"Of course, man. We'd love to have you still be a part of the wedding. It would suck if you weren't there. You're like a brother to us. We love Sean and we love you too."

"I'm very happy for you guys, but I don't think I could do it."

"Do what?" Mark asked.

"Get married."

"Why?"

"I just never thought about being married to a guy."

Mark cleared his throat, "Are you going to tell Sean what happened?"

Johnny was about to take another sip of his beer but put it back down on the bar. "You know, I was wondering when his name would come up in this conversation."

"It was inevitable. You know he still cares about you."

"Well, he has a funny way of showing it sleeping with Craig!"

"Well, you were no angel either, you know!"

"I didn't sleep with Tagger. We just kissed!"

"And that makes it better?"

Johnny scoffed and exhaled, "I don't want to talk about this so could we please change the subject and drink our free beers?"

Mark drank his beer as Johnny put out another cigarette. They sat there uncomfortable for a moment looking around the pub in silence.

That night, Sean met up with Michelle at the art gallery. He was helping her take down some art pieces and put up new ones for an upcoming show.

"So, let me get this straight, you're now dating Craig, you broke it off with Johnny and Jaime wants you back? Is that right?" Michelle said carrying a painting across the room.

"Yeah, that about covers it, but I'm not dating Craig, we're just seeing each other…. I guess," Sean mentioned slightly uncomfortable.

"Is there a difference?" Michelle picked up another painting and set it down against the wall, "Do you have feelings for Craig?"

Sean stopped, "Are you kidding? I'm still in love with Johnny!"

"Then why are you 'seeing' Craig and why did you sleep with him?"

Sean sighed and leaned against the wall, "I don't know. It all started with a kiss, then dinner, music, sweet-talking, and I hadn't heard from Johnny. I was a little upset and emotional. Craig made me feel good. He made me feel that everything would be alright."

Michelle grabbed her coffee from the counter and stood next to Sean, "And is everything alright? Is everything peachy?" Michelle said with a little sarcasm.

"Oh, shut up!"

Michelle laughed and took a sip of her coffee, "So tell me…sex with Craig…was it good?"

Sean giggled, "It was better than that."

"Better than Johnny?"

"No," Sean said quietly.

"Sean…"

"Michelle, it doesn't matter anymore. I made my bed, now I have to lie in it!"

"With Craig or Johnny?"

Sean scoffed, "Neither…Johnny probably happy as hell with Tagger."

"What, that guy that was singing to him at the party?"

"That would be the one."

"Now, that was some freaky shit."

"Tell me about it."

"I remember when Johnny used to write and sing YOU love songs."

"I know, and now I've become the cheating asshole."

"You *both* were in the wrong here. You just took it one step further."

"Thank you. That helps a lot."

Michelle leaned against the wall with Sean and put her arm around Sean, "You know, it's not too late to work things out with him."

"I think it is. He kicked me out of the apartment, which I don't blame him..."

"This can be fixed! You're sleeping in Craig's spare bedroom when you have a nice comfortable bedroom, bed, and apartment of your own...complete with a good man...who loves you and will forgive you..."

"How can you be so sure?"

"I've never seen you smile so much as when you were with Johnny. You both were so happy together."

"Craig makes me smile...and is there for me right now. He's very comfortable now..."

"What happens when that moment is over, and you need comforting in a different, yet familiar way?"

Sean didn't answer. He just looked the other way and Michelle grinned as she took another sip of her coffee. Sean's phone rang, and he got up to answer it. He walked across the gallery, then suddenly stopped, and dropped the phone to his side. Michelle noticed there was something wrong, "Sean? What's wrong?"

"Craig...he's in the hospital. He's been in an accident," Sean trembled.

Michelle ran behind the counter, grabbed her purse and keys, as they both ran out of the gallery, "Come on, I'll drive!"

It Comes Down To...

At the hospital, Craig was laid up with abrasions and a cast on his right leg. He was flipping through channels trying to find something else on television while a nurse was checking his IV and vital signs. There was a knock at the door. As the door opened, Johnny entered. He had a get-well card from the gift shop in his hand. Craig was surprised to see him after the scene at the tuxedo shop and the fact he slept with Sean. Even though Craig was confused as to why Johnny was there, at the same time he was glad. Johnny looked at Craig with his leg elevated and cuts on bruises on his face. He cleared his throat, "How are you doing?" Johnny said.

"I'm okay…" Craig said as he tried to sit up in the bed. Johnny walked around the bed and sat in the chair next to the bed. He gave Craig the card as the nurse smiled at them and left the room.

"So, what happened?" Johnny asked.

"I was surfing and……how did you know I was here?"

"Seth told me."

"Yeah, he came by earlier and brought me a burrito. I needed something else other than this hospital food," Craig pointed toward the sink area where his tray of scrumptious gourmet hospital food sat uneaten. Craig looked at Johnny strangely as Johnny was distracted by the television, "Not to sound rude, but why did you come? After the other day, I wouldn't say you and I were the closest of friends."

"Well, I know this is not the best time, but I wanted to come by to see how you were doing and apologize for my behavior. I'm sorry."

"There's no need for you to apologize. I should be the one apologizing to you."

"Look, I know about you and Sean and I'm okay with it. I guess you make him happy and that's what he needs. Just make sure he stays that way, okay? Johnny smiled, "He's been through a lot and needs a good man in his life; someone that will watch over him and be there for him. Just because it didn't work out with us doesn't mean it won't work for you two."

"Johnny, you're a good guy. I've seen a lot of change in Sean because of you. I wasn't trying to take him away from you. Please know that. I was just trying to be there for him as a friend and I did more harm than good…"

Johnny shook his head, "No, you're not to blame for this. This was all about us. We messed this up. You were just trying to be there for him, and I understand that."

"Sean will never love me as much as he loves you. I know that. I see that in his eyes," Craig said.

"I'm not going to forget the fact you slept with my boyfriend, but I'm not holding it against you either. It takes two, right?" Johnny joked.

Craig smiled at Johnny. Johnny held out his hand and Craig shook it. Craig suddenly noticed Johnny's swollen fingers and knuckles, "Dude, what happened to your hand?"

Johnny looked at his hand, "Oh, I quit the band."

"That must've been one hell of an exit interview!"

"Nah, just creative differences."

Craig grinned and realized this would be the perfect time to tell Johnny something that has been weighing on his mind. "Hey, there's something I should tell you."

"What?"

"It has to do with Jaime…"

"What about him?" Johnny said uninterested.

Craig adjusts himself in the bed, "You should know that he's planning on getting Sean back….by any means necessary."

Johnny confused, "Getting him back?"

"He wants to get back with Sean. I might have told him some information that he's using as ammunition against you....and his name is Tagger."

"Tagger? What does he have to do with this?"

"Jaime hired Tagger to join your band, get friendly with you, and seduce you so that it would break you and Sean up. Johnny, you must know that I didn't mean to tell him anything, but you know how Jaime is.... he had some information over me that could've proven to be harmful, but that doesn't matter anymore. What does matter is that Jaime's not through with you!"

"Well, Sean and I are no longer together. What else could he do?" Johnny asked confused.

"He wants to hurt you...completely take you out of the picture... and it's looking like he's stopping at nothing to make that happen."

"What more do you know, Craig? What's going to happen?"

"Jaime hired some guys to wait for you in the back entrance of Midnights after rehearsal to kick your ass."

"That's not a big deal since I'm no longer with the band..."

"Yeah, I know...but they did get Tagger. I guess that was part of Jaime's plan Tagger wasn't aware of."

"They beat up Tagger?" Johnny asked.

"Yeah, they got him pretty good. He's here in the hospital two floors down. Johnny, please forgive me. I should've never told Jaime anything about you and Sean. I should've kept my mouth shut and just dealt with what Jaime had in store for me."

"Craig. I don't blame you...considering what Jaime is capable of, you did what you had to do. Just glad you weren't hurt in all of this," Johnny pondered for a moment, "You know, I think Jaime has gone too far this time. I think it's about time I met up with Jaime, so he and I could talk.... man, to man.... New York style!"

Craig grinned and lay back on the bed with his arms behind his head.

A few days later, Jaime was leaving his apartment. He walked around the back of the building to the alley where his car was parked. As he walked down the alley to his car, he pulled the keys out of his pocket but dropped them on the ground. He bent down to pick them up and suddenly heard whistling and footsteps approaching him from behind. Jaime stood up nervous as the whistling became loud and clear.

Jaime froze, and the whistling stopped, "Take what you want, just please don't hurt me."

"Well, I can't make any promises," Johnny said as he stood behind Jaime holding a baseball bat.

Jaime recognized his voice and turned around to Johnny. He was relieved and smiled, "Well, if it isn't my old breeder friend, Johnny. How goes it?"

"You know, funny you should ask, I'm not doing so well. I'm a little down because I was stood up."

"Hot date?" Jaime smirked.

"Yeah, you can say that, but you see, it was a date you set up for me…"

Jaime suddenly looked confused as Johnny began playing with the bat he was holding, "Me? What do you mean?"

"Don't tell me you forgot? Tagger, the guy you hired to woo me and break Sean and me up. Don't you remember?"

Jaime nervously chuckled, "I have no idea what you're talking about…"

Johnny started to walk around Jaime still playing with the baseball bat, "Oh, of course, you do. See, you figured if we broke up, I would be out of the picture for a while which would leave you some room to move in on Sean. That was your plan, right? Am I close?"

"That's such bullshit," Jaime stuttered, "I'm over Sean. I dumped him, remember. Where would you get such a crazy idea?"

"Well, I have my sources…and my sources also told me that you had hired some goons to kick my ass after rehearsal. Well, you might have gotten away with that if I was still with the band. Tagger became the new lead singer as well as the proud owner of a *very* big hospital bill. Your goons kicked his ass and put him in a cast or two…"

Jaime's eyes got big and his jaw dropped. He started to walk away towards his car as Johnny followed, "I figure since you no longer had use for Tagger you needed to dispose of him as well…bravo! You just weren't able to dispose of me!" Johnny said getting a better grip on the bat.

"Oh, God…" Jaime said softly.

"Yeah, he's not going to be able to help you now," Johnny said getting angry, "You just sent a guy to the hospital!"

Jaime laughed and shrugged his shoulders, "What can I say? Accidents happen!"

Johnny grinned and gripped the bat, "You know, you're right about that because you're about to have one right now!"

Jaime stopped and extended his arms out to Johnny, "Johnny, come on, we can talk about this. There's no need to get ugly…"

Johnny pointed the bat at Jaime, "You have done nothing but inflict pain on those I know and love and now it's time for me to return that favor!"

"If this is about Natalie, man, I dumped her ass a long time ago…"

Johnny inhaled, "This is not just about Natalie, but I see you still wear that same shitty ass cologne!"

"Dude, I did you a favor…"

Johnny swung at Jaime with the bat with such force but missed on purpose. Jaime started to walk past his car down the alley towards the entrance of the road.

Johnny followed with the bat over his shoulder, "How the hell do you know what's good for me or anyone!!"

Jaime began to walk faster, and Johnny picked up the pace after him. The street entrance got closer as Jaime tried to reason with Johnny in every possible way, "Johnny, wait! We can talk about this. I've got money.... how much do you want? I can…"

"Save it!" Johnny shouted, "You can't say or buy your way out of this! You're an ugly and evil person and I'm about to do a lot a people a big favor, inflict pain on you as you have on everyone else, especially to the man I love!"

Johnny got ready to swing the bat when Jaime turned and ran into the street. He didn't notice the 4X4 truck approaching as he turned into its headlights. The blaring of the horn and the screeching of the tires drowned out the cry of fear that came from Jaime as the truck plunged into him knocking him out of his shoes and thirty yards back onto the pavement. The truck continued down the road avoiding running over Jaime lying in the street.

Johnny stood there in shock before dropping the bat and running to Jaime. Traffic came to a halt as drivers got out of their cars to see if they could help. People walking by stopped to see what happened as they talked amongst themselves. Someone screamed to call 911 as others gasped in shock at what happened. Johnny got to Jaime's mangled bloody body lifeless with his eyes still open as if he was still looking at the headlights approaching him. Johnny just stood there staring at Jaime in horror as the sound and lights of the ambulance approached, but there was nothing no one could do now for Jaime. A hit and run took the life of someone that everyone wished were dead. Even though it was sad, it seemed their wish had finally been granted.

The paramedics covered the body and Johnny walked away slowly still looking at the blood splatter not covered by the sheet. He looked to see Jaime's Prada loafers over by the curb, then back at the remains of Jaime. The coroner arrived shortly and put the body in a long, black bag into the back of the van. Johnny stopped as the coroner's van drove away along with the ambulance. The police stayed around the talk to witness to get a statement. A tear rolled down Johnny's cheek as he couldn't help but feel responsible for the death of Jaime Burns.

His funeral was scarcely attended, which was not a surprise to those who knew him, but according to those who attended, it was the social event of the year with big, expensive flowers surrounding the casket, his parents hired an orchestra and even though fewer than 10 people attended, the services took place in one of the biggest cathedrals in town. He was buried in a gold casket with platinum trim and in his favorite burnt grey Armani suit. Even in death, they still managed to make Jaime look better than those living and with a lot more bling.

Now What?

Three months had passed, and it had seemed a new season was vastly approaching. David and Mark got married and after the ceremony, Ally threw them a party on the rooftop of her building. Everyone was there to celebrate and congratulate the happy couple on their nuptials. Seamus, with his arm around Ally, stopped the music to make a toast to the couple. Ally and Seamus finally let their secret be known and was officially a couple in the eyes of their friends and family. They now were live together at Ally's place. A moving toast, the couple kissed, and the party continued. Some lights decorated the rooftop and a deejay playing countless 80's one-hit wonders. There was a dance floor in the middle surrounded by tables with paper lanterns and flowers of pink and magenta on each one.

Sean and Craig sat at one of the tables dressed in tuxedos watching people dance and sipping on champagne. Sean and Craig moved in with one another after they graduated from college. They were not a couple since Sean slept in the spare bedroom.

"What a night," Craig said as he looked out onto the dance floor.

"Yeah, I'm happy for them," Sean mentioned looking at David and Mark slow dancing in the middle of the floor even though an upbeat Human League song was playing.

"You think that will be you someday?"

"What married? I'm not sure…I would like to." Sean remarked.

"Anything is possible, right?"

Just then, Sean looked over to where Seth and Johnny were sitting. They sat there in tuxedos drinking beer instead of champagne. Johnny and Seth began writing spoken word poetry and performing at bars and coffee shops around town. They still want to put another band together but felt this was another way of expressing themselves and their talents. They seemed to have found another untapped market and a new fan base.

"I guess so," Sean said as he looked down at his champagne glass. Craig moved closer and hesitantly tried to hold Sean's hand, but Sean pulled away, "Craig, don't…"

"I'm sorry…I can't help it though. I know we're just friends, but I can't help the way I feel about you. I've been there for you, have given you space because I know this is a tough time for you, but do you think you should move on…maybe with me?"

"Craig, I can only offer you friendship. I do appreciate you being there for me and giving me a place to crash, but I am still in love with Johnny. If there is any possible way of getting him back, I would like to try." Sean looked across the floor at Johnny again. Ally and Seamus had joined them at their table. Johnny looked sad but caught Sean's eye.

Seth noticed and addressed Johnny, "Hey, why don't you go and talk to him?"

Johnny finished his beer, "No…"

"For months, you've been sulking about Sean and what happened to Jaime. You can't do anything about Jaime, but you can do something about Sean. He's right there. Go talk to the man."

A slow song began as people began to couple-up on the dance floor and some got up from their tables to join them, including Ally and Seamus. Sean put his arm around Craig, "Hey, strong and handsome, you want to dance?"

"Why don't you ask Johnny to dance?"

"Because I'm asking you…"

"He is who you want to dance with," Craig sighed, "So go and ask him, and while you're at it, talk to him…"

Sean sat there for a moment and then looked over at Johnny staring back at him. He put his glass down and got up from the table slowly. He walked across the floor moving in between couples dancing. Johnny straightens himself up as he notices Sean approaching.

"Hey Seth, how are you?" Sean asked.

"I'm good. How are you doing, Sean?"

"Can't complain…"

Sean and Seth looked at Johnny looking down at the table avoiding eye contact.

"Johnny?" Sean said.

"Yeah?" Johnny said quietly.

Sean cleared his throat, "Would you like to dance?" Sean held out his hand to Johnny. Johnny looked at it, then up at Sean. He looked at Seth as if he had the answer to Sean's question. Seth winked and smiled at Johnny. Johnny nodded his head, 'yes' to Sean. Johnny took Sean's hand firmly as Sean lead him to the dance floor. As they started to dance, Craig came to the table and sat next to Seth, "So what do you think?"

"I think you're going to have to find another roommate, my friend."

Craig smiled, "I knew they would get back together eventually…was kind of hoping for later…*much* later.

Seth drank his beer, "They just had to stop being stupid and find one another again." Just then, Michelle, wearing a very stunning black cocktail dress, came over to the table, leaned down, and kissed Seth on the lips. "Wanna dance, handsome?" Michelle was now the assistant manager of the gallery. Her life seemed to be moving forward. She's happy and now dating the man that admired her years prior; Seth. What started as friends with benefits was now Seth writing poetry about her and performing it in front of her and a crowd of strangers. So, it's safe to say that Seth was no longer interested in his ex-girlfriend, Kelly.

"You bet your ass I do!" Seth got up and wrapped his arms around Michelle leading her to the dance floor. Craig sat there alone at the table. Looking around, he took Seth's glass and drank the rest of his beer. He saw Sean and Johnny dancing on the floor and looking very uncomfortable. They were dancing as if they were strangers.

"How are you?" Sean said as he cleared his throat.

"I'm fine and you?"

"I'm fine…"

"That's good…"

"Good…"

Johnny accidentally stepped on Sean's toe, "I'm sorry."

"It's cool…we made a mess of things, huh?"

"Yeah, we sure did," Johnny snickered.

Another slow song came on and they continued to dance. This time they dance a little bit closer and more comfortable than during the first song.

"So, how's Tagger? Sean asked.

When Tagger got out of the hospital after the beating, the band didn't have the impact it did when Johnny and Seth were with it and disbanded. Tagger tried finding other bands to join, but they weren't impressed with what Tagger had to offer. He went back to whoring himself on the same corner where Jaime picked him up before moving to Oregon to live with his sister.

"I don't know and don't care."

"I heard what happened with the band. I'm sorry."

"Thanks, but we seem to be doing well with the spoken word thing…"

"I heard…congratulations!"

"Thank you…." Johnny looked at Sean, "So what are your plans now that you've graduated?"

Sean looked back into Johnny's eyes, "I think I'm going to look into writing a column for the paper, but in the meantime, take some time to myself. It's been a little crazy for me lately. I wish you could've been there to see me graduate…"

"I was there…"

Sean surprised, "You were?"

"I sent you the flowers after the ceremony." Johnny laughed. "I had to pay the usher twenty bucks!"

"I didn't know…"

"You weren't supposed to know. I told him not to tell you. I wouldn't be able to forgive myself if I didn't come and see my baby…. I mean…you graduate."

Sean smiled, "Do you still think of me as your 'baby'?"

"I never stopped…" Johnny grinned.

"I miss you," Sean exhaled.

Johnny exhaled, "I miss you too."

They both became teary-eyed before kissing one another intensely.

"Come home…" Johnny whispered.

"I'm already packed!" Sean smiled. They started to leave the dance floor as Sean held on to Johnny, "Wait, wait, do you have any plans next week?"

Johnny stopped, "Not that I know of, why?"

"Well, my cousin gave me two train tickets to Sonoma as a graduation present."

"A romantic train ride to wine country. Who are you taking with you?" Johnny smirked.

"Hmmm, I was thinking about taking someone special."

"Craig?" Johnny joked.

"No, someone else and I think you know this guy…he's likes to dance in his underwear to a particular Amy Grant song that I love." Sean teased.

"I hate Amy Grant," Johnny whispered with a grin. They laughed and left the dance floor. Johnny and Sean immediately went to Craig's place and got Sean's stuff

Later that night in a dream, Sean put both of his hands on the bathroom sink and looked at himself in the mirror. It was completely dark in the bathroom except for the light above Sean's head. He turned on the cold water, stuck his hands under the faucet and splashed water on his face. He opened his eyes and continued to look at himself in the mirror. He could hear his heart pound in his chest. The cordless phone on the sink rang three times. Sean reached for the phone but couldn't seem to reach it. It rang three more times.

Sean just stared at the phone still extending to reach it and noticed his wrist cut and bleeding. As the blood gushed from his wrist into the sink, someone's hand came up from behind, grabbed his wrist, and squeezed it tightly securing the bleeding. Sean's heart pounded even faster than before. Sean was startled and wanted to scream but couldn't. He felt the touch of soft lips on the back of his neck. He closed his eyes as the phone rang again three times. Sean arched his head back and to the right, but another hand came across Sean's face moving his fingers across his lips. A comforting face came into view in the dim light.

"Am I dreaming?" Sean said breathing heavily.

"Yes...so let the machine get it." Johnny whispered in Sean's ear. Sean exhaled and grinned. As Johnny began nibbling on Sean's ear, the phone stopped ringing.